THE MAN, THE MYTH

A TANNER NOVEL - BOOK 24

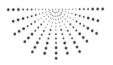

REMINGTON KANE

Year Zero

INTRODUCTION

THE MAN, THE MYTH – A TANNER NOVEL - BOOK 24

The consequences of Tanner's momentous decision make themselves known, as an enemy seeks to use a surrogate to destroy him.

Meanwhile, members of the law enforcement think tank Blue Truth delve into the century-old mystery of the assassin named Tanner, as they seek to discover if he's a man or a mere myth.

ACKNOWLEDGMENTS

I write for you.

—Remington Kane

PROLOGUE

CHICAGO, ILLINOIS

ON THE THIRTY-FIFTH FLOOR OF A GLASS TOWER WERE THE offices of a corporation calling itself Solution Allies. The company's motto stated their mission—We serve the customer and fulfill their every need.

While the slogan's sentiments were sincere and expressed the organization's true intent, their identity as Solution Allies was a facade. Solution Allies went by another name, Ordnance Inc., and one of their latest customers was not feeling as if his needs had been fulfilled.

Jared Harkness paced in the reception area that was adjacent to Trevor Healy's office. Harkness had recently contracted Ordnance Inc. to locate, abduct, and obtain information from a man named Duke Philips. Harkness sought to take over Duke's role as the main supplier of high-ticket black-market items in New York City. To do so, he needed Duke's contacts and client list.

To that end, Harkness had contracted with Ordnance

Inc. to handle the job. A short time later, his money was returned to his account and the contract cancelled with no reason given. Incensed and confused by the refusal of his business, Harkness phoned Trevor Healy, whom he once worked beside at Hexalcorp and considered a friend. He was unable to reach Healy and was told that, "Mr. Healy would call him back at his earliest convenience."

Desiring to talk to the man in person, Harkness boarded a plane to Chicago. He'd spent the last two hours stewing in Healy's reception area while the haughty blonde behind the desk did her best to ignore him. On his arrival, she had called Healy and told him that Harkness had come to Chicago to see him. Healy asked her to tell Harkness that he would be back at the building soon and to wait for him.

As he was about to bother the receptionist again, the door behind Harkness opened and revealed Trevor Healy.

"Trevor, it's about damn time you got here."

Healy smiled at him. "I'm a busy man these days, Jared. I just returned yesterday from a trip to Mexico and next week I'm due to head back there again."

"Why the hell did you cancel my contract?"

Healy held up a finger, urging patience. "We'll talk in my office."

After stopping at the desk to gather messages and news from the receptionist, Healy went into his office with Harkness tagging along behind him. Harkness was three steps into the massive space when his jaw dropped open. Healy's office had an envious view of Chicago's famed Loop area and the Chicago River beyond it. It contained a wet bar, a large seating area, and a conference table that could accommodate eighteen.

"Holy Crap, Trevor, this office is twice the size of my apartment."

Healy smiled proudly as he placed his laptop bag on his hand-carved oak desk.

"I'm the executive coordinator now, Jared, second only to Grayson Talbot. I told you to join us when Hexalcorp spun us off into a separate enterprise. If you had, you wouldn't be dealing with that petty problem of yours."

"If it's such a petty problem why did you refuse to help me with it? Does Duke Philips have some sort of pull with Ordnance Inc.?"

"Duke is a flea, a nobody, but he's under the protection of someone that requires special handling."

"Who?"

"The assassin named Tanner."

Harkness settled into one of the plush seats that were in front of Healy's desk. "Tanner is a friend of Duke Philips? That certainly changes things."

"I don't know how friendly they are, but Tanner called me and asked that we not get involved. I agreed."

"Why?"

"Tanner and Ordnance Inc. had dealings in the past and we declared a truce. I'm not willing to violate the cease-fire agreement at this time."

"I heard about that setback you guys had in Texas some time ago. Was that Tanner?"

Healy nodded. "It's a secret, so keep it to yourself, but yeah, the bastard took out a Hammer Team and killed others. I'm only alive because he wasn't in the mood to murder me. The man will pay in blood for everything he's done, but not until we're ready to deal with him."

"I guess that means I'm shit out of luck when it comes to taking over Manhattan's black-market."

Healy smiled. "I have an idea that may solve both our problems, but I warn you, if it fails, Tanner will come after you."

Harkness crossed one leg over the other. "I'm listening."

"Have you ever heard of the Magic Man?"

"What is he, a magician?"

"He's an assassin, no, that's wrong, he's a facilitator of assassinations. The Magic Man has been responsible for coming up with ways to take out some of the toughest targets. We recently used his services to help us with a project in South America. Eight different assassins had failed to kill a Bolivian businessman, while being eliminated by his security forces. Thanks to the Magic Man, we accomplished the task with ease."

"How does he work?"

Healy spoke while leaving his desk, to move over to the bar. "The man is a master at taking a target's strength and turning it into a weakness that can be exploited. I've asked him to look into Tanner."

Harkness had followed Healy over to the bar, where he requested a Scotch on ice. After taking his first sip, he made an observation.

"You want me to be the one who takes the flak if this Magic Man guy fails to kill Tanner."

"That's right. None of this can be tied back to Ordnance Inc."

"Okay, let's say I agree to throw in with this Magic Man character, what's it cost me?"

"Not a dime, Jared, although, it could amount to losing your life if it doesn't work out."

"Tanner is one tough bastard to kill. The word on the street is that even the mob decided to make peace with him instead of going to war."

Trevor waved a hand at that. "The mafia is a dying organization. Meanwhile, Ordnance Inc. has more than tripled in size in a year. If the Magic Man doesn't kill

Tanner, we will, but my boss wants more time to prepare before we commit to that. When we do go after the son of a bitch, we'll be an overwhelming force."

"You say that, but I know you, Trevor. You're not a patient man. You want to go after Tanner now, don't you?"

"That's where you come in."

"And if I'm successful, it will save you the trouble and expense of launching a massive attack, while also making you look good, eh?"

"That's right, so, what do you say?"

"Sweeten the deal with a million-dollar bonus and we have an agreement."

Healy held out his hand. "If you succeed in killing Tanner, I'll see that you get two-million."

Harkness smiled as he shook Healy's hand. "It's a deal. When can this Magic Man get to New York?"

"Oh, the guy never leaves his house. His assistant, Dwight, does all the leg work. Like I said before, the Magic Man thinks of himself as a facilitator, a master tactician, and he's never failed."

Harkness snorted. "What sort of guy goes around calling himself Magic Man?"

"A pompous ass," Healy said. "But if he kills Tanner for me, hell, I'll kiss his ass."

The men laughed, clinked their glasses together, then went on to work out the details of their plan.

1

THE RETURN OF CODY PARKER

STARK, TEXAS, THE PARKER RANCH

CODY PARKER KNELT DOWN IN FRONT OF THE GRAVES OF his family and spoke to them in a quiet voice. Having no way of knowing if they would ever hear him... somehow. His words were not for them, but rather, they were a vow he was making to himself.

He had come home to Stark, reclaimed his identity, and regained their land. With Sara as his wife, they would have children, and give new life to the Parker family. He was Cody again, after so many years of living under aliases, and he liked being Cody Parker.

The town of Stark had considered the Parker family extinct. The revelation that Cody Parker had survived, and that he was back, had electrified the town. Add to that the existence of Caleb Parker, an unknown younger brother to Cody, and the Parkers were the biggest thing to happen to Stark since the massacre that nearly ended them.

After leaving the family cemetery, Cody headed back

toward the house while dodging puddles. The area had suffered from a lack of precipitation for decades but the last few days had seen several inches of rain come down with a massive storm on the horizon.

As he reached the top step of his front porch, Cody's phone alerted him that he had a visitor. Someone had turned onto the entrance to the driveway and activated motion detectors and cameras.

Cody looked down at his phone screen. A camera hidden inside a fence post transmitted video of the driver behind the wheel of a yellow sports car, which was a Fiat Spider. A grin formed on Cody's face. After putting away his phone, he walked down the steps to meet his guest.

The young woman who emerged from the car was shapely and beautiful. Her long dark hair glistened, and her brown skin was glowing with vitality. Instead of issuing words of greeting, she walked up to Cody, wrapped her arms around him, and kissed him fully on the mouth.

Sara had also been alerted to the young woman's arrival. She stood behind them in the home's open doorway with a scowl darkening her face.

"I hope you have a good reason for kissing that girl."

The kiss ended as the young woman looked past Cody. "She's Sara?"

"That's Sara."

"She's beautiful, Tanner."

"Yes, she is, and remember, I'm Cody Parker now."

"I know, and the whole town is talking about your return. Don't worry though, I can keep a secret."

Sara walked down the stairs to join them, and Tanner made the introductions.

"Romina Reyes, meet Sara Blake, soon to be Mrs. Sara Parker."

"Oh, this is Romina?" Sara said. "It's nice to finally meet you."

"Mom said you were beautiful, Sara. I see she was right."

"Thank you, and you're gorgeous. I was jealous watching that kiss."

Romina patted Cody's cheek. "I've had a crush on your fiancé for years."

Cody first met Romina Reyes after returning to Stark for the first time after a long absence. Romina, who at the time was sixteen, lived with her mother and older brother. They had made their home on the land that had been the birthplace of Cody Parker, and the site of the Parker family massacre. At the time, Romina knew Cody as Tanner.

Maria Reyes, Romina's mother, married Chuck Willis. Willis had moved himself and his business to the town from San Antonio and had helped to revitalize the area. He also owned land adjacent to what was once again the Parker ranch, and that made Romina a neighbor.

"Is your mother here too, Romina?" Cody asked.

"Mom sent her apologies, but no, she and Chuck are still in France, something about a business deal taking longer than expected."

"And what about Chaz Willis?"

"Chaz?"

"Your boyfriend."

Romina laughed. "We broke up two years ago, Tan— uh, Cody. Besides, when Mom married his father, Chaz became my stepbrother. Dating your stepbrother would seem creepy to me."

"It's his loss," Cody said.

Doc came walking over from the area of the stables. He lit up in a huge grin when he saw who their visitor was.

"Romina, how are you, honey?"

"I'm good, Doc," Romina said, as she went to the old man and hugged him. When she released Doc, Romina walked back over to her car. "I just stopped by to meet Sara, but I'll be home most of the summer."

"Can't you stay a little longer?" Sara asked.

"I'd like to, but I'm supposed to meet up with a few of my old friends and I'm running late."

"Okay, and it was nice to meet you," Sara said.

"Same here," Romina said. After a wave and a smile, she drove off to visit her old classmates.

"That girl is a heartbreaker," Doc said.

Sara laughed. "When I came out onto the porch and saw her kissing Cody, I thought she was someone else."

"Who?" Cody asked.

"That Tonya Jennings you told me about. The one who figured out you were really Cody Parker."

"Tonya and that wimp of a husband of hers moved out of town, Sara," Doc said. "I think they're in Dallas."

"That suits me fine," Sara said, before asking Doc a question. "Did you check on my horse?"

"Yeah, and I see what you mean about Misty not looking well. My guess is that it's colic, but you might want to get a vet out here to examine her. In the meantime, I'll feed her a little fresh grass to see if that helps."

"Who is the vet around here these days, Doc?" Cody asked.

"It was old Cal Murphy, but he retired last month. The new doc is a lady named Alexander. The word is she's good, but I've never met her. I'll call Dr. Alexander's office and find out if she has time to come out today."

"Do that, and thanks."

As Doc went off to make a call, Cody took Sara's hand as they walked up the steps. They sat together on a porch swing while gazing out at acres of land that belonged to Cody and had been home to the Parker family for generations.

"I've got bad news," Sara said.

"What is it?"

"I've received an email message from a Blue Truth representative named Victor Middleton. He and his associates want to interview me. It concerns their investigation into the Tanner legend."

"Have you responded?"

"No, I wasn't sure how you wanted to play this."

"Agree to the interview. We'll be going back to New York City in a few days. They can meet with you there."

"And how should I handle it?"

"Tell them that you were convinced that Tanner was a lone man, then later came to believe that it was a name used by a number of assassins. As for the man you once pursued, you have reason to believe he died years ago."

"How should I say he died?"

"You'll have to make up a story. Maybe choose an accident victim who went unidentified."

"That makes sense; I'll do a little research before I speak to Blue Truth. I still don't like it that they're looking into you."

"Not me, Tanner. From now on, Tanner is a part I play when I'm out to fulfill a contract. I'm Cody Parker again, really Cody Parker again, and we're going to build a life here."

Sara leaned against Cody while laying her head on his shoulder. "Are we going to make this happen? I mean, separating your work from your everyday life?"

"We are, and I won't be the first Tanner to have done so. Tanner Three, Benjamin Boudreaux, he ran a farm and raised a family while being a Tanner. I've always admired the man and sought to be like him. Thanks to the memoir he left behind in the Book of Tanner, I'll know some of the pitfalls to watch out for."

"Such as?"

"Keep the lives separate, always, and destroy anyone who threatens your home."

"Ordnance Inc. could threaten us… and they likely will someday."

Cody took in a deep breath and released it in a huff of air. "I know, and logic tells me to strike first and end the threat."

"But you gave your word to let them be as long as they returned the favor."

"Yes."

"And a Tanner never goes back on his word."

"That's right, and neither does a Parker."

"Despite the risk we're taking, I want you to leave them alone. Nothing is worth losing your honor over."

"Sara, if they do come someday, I want you to know that I'll—"

"—Protect us, you'll protect us and kill them all, and once you do, no one will dare to come at us again."

"I love you, Sara."

"And I love you too, Cody."

"Does it still feel strange to call me by that name?"

"A little, but I like it, and I'll love calling you husband too."

Cody Parker smiled. It felt damn good to be home.

2

THE FATES CONSPIRE

HOUSTON, TEXAS

Caleb had been staying at the ranch but needed to fly back to his other home in California. Caleb co-owned a farm with his sister, Sadie Knox. His plan was to stay at the farm for a few days before heading back to the ranch. Now that it was common knowledge in Stark that he was a Parker, the ranch felt as much like home to him as the farm he'd grown up on.

His flight had a short layover in Houston, and being a weekday afternoon, the plane wasn't crowded. There were more than a few rows of seats with no one using them, which is why it surprised Caleb when a woman took the seat beside him.

When pursuing thieves as Stark, Caleb preferred to dress in a three-piece suit and don a fedora. He was traveling as himself and so he was wearing jeans and a black short-sleeved shirt. Despite the change in attire, the woman who slid into the seat next to him had recognized him at a glance. When Caleb turned his head to look at her, he was startled.

"Dr. Mao?"

Jen Mao grinned at Caleb. "Hello, Stark."

Along with Tanner, Caleb had rescued Dr. Jennifer Mao from a burning house days earlier. She'd been barricaded in a room to die by one of the team of home invaders who had kidnapped her for her medical skills. Although he'd felt an attraction for the doctor, which seemed mutual, Caleb never thought he'd see her again. He looked about the plane while wondering if FBI Agent Eriksen was somehow responsible for Jen's appearance.

"Relax," Jen said, "I'm here alone. I've decided to leave Laredo and I'm flying home to California to look for an apartment."

Caleb settled back in his seat. "Did you talk to anyone about me, Doctor?"

Jen frowned as she remembered the conversation she'd had in the hospital with Agent Eriksen.

"A female FBI agent figured out that you were involved in rescuing me from the fire those home invaders had set."

"Was her name Eriksen?"

"How did you know?"

"It was an educated guess. What did you tell her?"

"I told her the truth, that you risked your life to save me."

"And what about the man I was with? Did she ask about him?"

"No, she was under the impression that you always worked alone."

"I do, normally."

Jen leaned in closer and whispered. "Eriksen said that you were a vigilante who liked to hunt down thieves. Is that true?"

"Guilty."

"That sounds dangerous."

"It can be, but I can't stand it when men like Wicks and his crew think they can just do whatever they want and get away with it, so I take from the takers."

Jen kissed him on the cheek. "You also saved this damsel when she was in distress."

Caleb returned her smile.

Jen leaned closer, then pulled up his left sleeve. There was a bandage on Caleb's arm. It covered the burn he'd received while rescuing Jen. "How's that injury coming along?"

"It's almost healed, thanks to the care you gave it."

"It was the least I could do," Jen said, as they stared into each other's eyes.

Then, it was time for the flight attendants to prepare everyone for takeoff. Once they had given the safety speech for the ten-thousandth time, Caleb asked Jen where in California she was looking to settle down. To his surprise, she named a town that was a short drive from where his farm was located.

"Do you know the area, Stark?"

"I do… I live near there."

Jen's smile was brilliant as she said, "Really? It must be fate."

They continued to talk during the flight and laughed often. If fate was trying to throw them together, Caleb was grateful.

3

THE MAGIC MAN

SEATTLE, WASHINGTON

THE MAGIC MAN WAS A FORTY-NINE-YEAR-OLD FORMER psychiatrist named Jonathon Baxter. Baxter was portly, wore glasses, and was a student of human behavior. The Magic Man was someone who had always believed he was the smartest kid in the class; more often than not, he had been.

Baxter began offering his services as the Magic Man three years earlier, after reading an article about a failed assassination attempt on a St. Louis mobster.

Details of the attempt made it into the news and Baxter became intrigued. Having used his great intellect to amass a fortune and retire early, Baxter was bored. He decided to devise an assassination plan that would work.

So captivated was he with the idea that he flew to St. Louis to look over the area where the mobster lived. After the attempt on his life, it was said the man never left his home. With the help of a private eye, Baxter had gathered information on the hoodlum's private life and habits. Within a day, Baxter had what he thought was a foolproof plan to assassinate the target. However, he had no way to prove it.

That was when he reached out to a former patient of his, Dwight Wheatley. Dwight was a sociopath whom Baxter had treated when he was a teen. The word "treatment" was a misnomer. Sociopaths couldn't be cured, only understood and accepted.

Dwight's parents were worried about the boy's lack of empathy toward others and his inability to display affection to them. Baxter knew what Dwight was after speaking to him for one session. In their next meeting, he made a suggestion to the boy.

"Give your parents what they want."

"Why should I?"

"Two reasons. One, they'll bother you less, and two, you might find it fun to pretend."

The teen had been pacing in front of Baxter's desk. He settled into the leather wing chair in front of it and grinned at Baxter.

"You're recommending I lie to my parents?"

"You are what you are, a sociopath. You'll never experience the emotions they want you to feel, but you can fake them enough to satisfy their needs. By nourishing their desires, they'll be more inclined to leave you at peace and to buy you things you want. I'd say that's a win-win."

Dwight had agreed to try it. He discovered that Baxter had been right. Not only did his parents become easier to deal with, but it was fun pretending to give a damn about them. Dwight and his father never argued again, and when he turned seventeen the man bought him a new car.

As for Dr. Baxter, he had gained a weekly appointment with Dwight that paid well. While the teen was in his office, he caught up on paperwork while Dwight played with a hand-held video game. During the years the arrangement lasted, the two became friendly.

AT THE TIME BAXTER REACHED OUT TO DWIGHT FOR HIS help, the young man had just turned twenty-two. Dwight was making his living as an investigator for a sleazy attorney in Portland. He also did the occasional heist on the side and knew the sort of people Baxter hoped to make contact with. The two had dinner together in Seattle to discuss Baxter's dilemma.

"Why not whack the guy yourself, Jonathon?"

"I would be putting myself at risk; I'm also not a killer. Despite that, for my own satisfaction, I need to know if this plan will work."

"You've got money, hire a hitter and give him your plan."

"You know such men?"

"I know guys who can get in contact with one, yeah. Or better yet, we could try pitching the plan to the guy in St. Louis who wants the mobster dead."

"He's a rival hoodlum."

"There are guys here in Seattle who could get word to him and let him know you have a way to kill his enemy."

"That sounds like I'd be putting myself at risk."

"Do you care if you get paid?"

"No, I only want to know if my plan is feasible. It's become an obsession with me."

"Offer the plan for free and see if they bite. If it works, they'll love you."

Baxter thought that over while sipping on wine. With a grin he told Dwight, "Do it."

~

WITH HIS FIRST PLAN A SUCCESS, BAXTER WENT TO WORK designing strategies to assassinate other tough targets. The key was to fit the plan to the target. Baxter was a master at taking someone's strength and turning it into a weakness. Others then exploited that weakness and eliminated the target.

Bored with retirement and excited by the work, Baxter embarked on a new career. Dwight was his assistant. Over the three years they had worked together, Baxter, who went by the ego-enhancing appellation Magic Man, had acquired a stable of private investigators to gather information. There were also a number of assassins he could deploy to take down targets for clients. His second career was a lucrative one, and he found that he enjoyed the role of criminal mastermind.

Their current target was close to home and a resident of Seattle. He was Dale Rupert, a defense attorney who had recently lost a noteworthy case. Rupert's client had murdered his wife inside their home in a fit of rage. Despite the impressive list of forensic evidence the state accumulated against him, the client refused to accept the plea bargain arrangement offered by the King County Prosecuting Attorney.

He'd paid his lawyer, Dale Rupert, a small fortune to keep him from spending the rest of his life behind bars. In the end, the man had been found guilty by a jury and sentenced by a judge to forty years in a maximum-security prison. It was not the outcome the client had been hoping for and he blamed Rupert.

Dale Rupert handled many high-profile murder cases. Although he won far more often than he lost, he had let more than one rich client down over the years. Rupert had once been attacked by a knife-wielding assailant after he'd failed to keep the woman's husband from going to prison. Since then, he has gone out in public with two bodyguards and had taken other security precautions, such as wearing a bulletproof vest.

The attorney was a man who craved order and precision. Every day of his life was mapped out to the minute to achieve the maximum amount of efficiency and usefulness. Once the Magic Man became aware of this need in Rupert, which was one of the attorney's strengths, he devised a way to use it against him.

DWIGHT CHECKED THE TIME ON HIS CELL PHONE AND SAW that he had arrived at his first destination early. That was good. The Magic Man had a busy day planned for him and he didn't want to fall behind. He was in the parking garage beneath an apartment building near Seattle. One of the two personal bodyguards employed by Rupert lived in the building. Dwight was there to make certain the man arrived late for work.

After taking out a knife, Dwight pierced the sidewall on a rear tire of the bodyguard's ride. Even if he had a viable spare in the car's trunk, the delay would still work. The Magic Man had learned that the bodyguard took his daughter to school every morning before driving to Rupert's estate to report for work. The delay would not only annoy the target but also one of the men responsible for guarding the mark. Annoyed and agitated people made mistakes.

With his first chore accomplished, Dwight left the parking garage and headed back to where he'd parked the vehicle he was using. It was an old rust-riddled pickup truck.

Seeing that he had enough time to grab breakfast, Dwight stopped at a fast-food restaurant and fueled up on eggs, bacon, and hash browns. After getting a second cup of coffee to go, Dwight drove the ancient pickup truck onto Interstate 5 and joined the thickening morning traffic flowing into Seattle's downtown area. His goal was to make the traffic even worse.

After bringing the truck to a stop in the far right lane, Dwight removed the key and popped open the hood. It took less than a minute to disable the vehicle by disconnecting and removing the distributer cap. After tossing the plastic component into the other lanes of traffic, where it would be crushed by the flow of vehicles, Dwight walked away.

A short stroll along the shoulder of the road brought him to an on ramp that was filled with vehicles waiting to merge. Dwight walked passed them going the opposite way until he was on a city street. Another two minutes of walking and he arrived at the second vehicle he would be using that day, a motorcycle.

After getting on the bike, Dwight sped off to his third assignment. On the interstate, the abandoned pickup truck was doing its job well; the blocked lane caused the usual morning congestion to worsen.

INSTEAD OF PARKING ON THE STREET AND WALKING IN, Dwight decided to ride the motorcycle onto the playground area of the elementary school. This delighted the children and irritated their parents and teachers.

After bringing the bike to a halt near a group of eight-year-old girls, Dwight spotted his victim talking to another child near a yellow sliding board. Dwight coasted the bike over to the little girl and stared at her through the tinted glass of his helmet. The little blonde girl was what most people would think of as adorable. To Dwight, she was nothing more than an assignment. He had memorized her face the night before and knew he had the right child. Rearing back his gloved fist, he delivered a punch to the girl's mouth. The youngster fell backwards, hit the ground, and began wailing.

Dwight took off on the bike, weaved around a woman who was foolish enough to step in front of him, and was soon merged into the morning traffic. Beneath his helmet, Dwight was smiling. He had completed three out of four tasks and the last one didn't need to be done for hours. He headed home to play a new video game he'd bought the day before.

In the school playground, the little girl had suffered a split lip and had a loosened front tooth. For the rest of her life she would feel uneasy around men on motorcycles.

DALE RUPERT WAS HAVING A BAD DAY. FIRST, ONE OF HIS bodyguards delayed his departure from his fortress of a home by arriving late. Rupert was annoyed, but since he allowed time in his schedule for a small delay, he assumed he would still arrive to the office on time. That assessment was wrong.

Some idiot had driven his piece of crap pickup truck onto the interstate and broken down. By the time the abandoned vehicle had been towed away, Rupert had already become a victim of it and arrived at work twelve minutes late. It put him off-schedule and ruined his mood.

To top things off, his personal assistant received a call from her child's school. Some miscreant had struck his assistant's daughter in the face, then ridden off on a motorcycle. As much as he wanted to insist that she stay at work, Rupert agreed that the woman had to leave and see to her daughter. The law clerk who took her place was competent enough but having to explain things to him wasted more time. In order to get back on track, Rupert had to postpone a conference call. He had an important dinner meeting with a client who was an hour away in Olympia and couldn't afford to show up late for it.

Rupert had prepared by bringing a change of clothes to the office, so that he wouldn't have to go back home first and take a chance of running into bad traffic. After showering and shaving, Rupert changed in his private bathroom. Feeling refreshed and on track again, he was ready to go. With his bodyguards beside him, Rupert pressed the call button on his private elevator. It was a few seconds before he realized that the doors weren't opening and that there was a problem.

DOWN IN THE SUB-BASEMENT LEVEL OF THE OFFICE building, Dwight had completed his last task of the day. He had severed wires that were vital to the operation of Rupert's personal elevator. With his last chore done, Dwight went off to have dinner with the Magic Man. If everything worked out as planned, Dale Rupert would be dead by the time Dwight arrived.

Rupert jammed a thumb against the elevator's call button several more times before giving up. With a grunt of frustration, he looked at his watch, then headed for the door that led to the corridor.

"I'll have to take one of the regular elevators," Rupert told his bodyguards. "Since it's the end of the day, there will probably be a wait for the damn things."

The two beefy men hurried to keep up with their slender boss as he marched down the hallway. As Rupert was passing a window, the glass exploded inward. The supersonic round that caused it entered Rupert's temple and killed him.

On the roof of a nearby building, one of the Magic Man's assassins disassembled his weapon and placed it in its carrying case. He was a handsome man and well-dressed in a tailored suit. Two minutes later, he was riding a crowded elevator down to the ground-floor along with the accountants and dentists who populated the building.

As the group left the elevator and walked out onto the street, the sound of an approaching siren could be heard. The assassin shared a taxi with a lovely young dental technician as the first police car arrived on the scene.

Rupert's obsession to be on time had been combined with a frustrating day. The result was that he left the protection of his bodyguards behind as he rushed to leave the building.

The assassin, who was named Fontaine, smiled. He had been tracking Rupert for over a week and had only caught glimpses of the man. Rupert arrived to work each day in a bulletproof limo, parked it in an enclosed space, then would take a private elevator up to his office. While he would eventually appear in court without his bodyguards beside him, trying to hit him there would have been too dangerous. Luring him out into the corridor of his office building was brilliant.

The dental assistant noticed the satisfied smile the assassin wore. "Why the grin?"

"Oh, I was just thinking of my boss; the man is a genius."

"That's funny; most people hate their bosses."

"Mine makes my job easier," said Fontaine, then he suggested that they stop somewhere and have a drink. The woman agreed, and later that night, Fontaine bedded her. All in all, a very good day. That is, if your name wasn't Dale Rupert.

4

ONCE A BADASS, ALWAYS A BADASS

STARK, TEXAS, THE PARKER RANCH

THE RANCH RECEIVED A SECOND VISITOR AS CHIEF OF Police Steven Mendez drove his marked SUV onto the property. Sara was over at the barn awaiting the arrival of the veterinarian, so Cody walked out to greet the chief alone.

The fact that Steve Mendez had become a cop surprised Cody. Mendez had a wild streak when he was a teen and had a habit of getting into fistfights. Cody had always liked him, and they had been friends since grade school.

Mendez was dressed in jeans along with a black long-sleeved T-shirt, which was tucked inside his pants. His erect posture and muscular build told you the man was in good shape. His eyes took in his surroundings as he swiveled his head while he walked. Although he looked Caucasian, the chief's father was of Mexican descent, and Mendez had been born in Stark. His duty weapon was positioned on his left hip alongside a gold badge that identified him as the chief of police of Stark.

The chief greeted Cody with a smile as he shook his head in amazement.

"It still blows my mind that you're alive, Cody."

"I guess it would. How are you, Steve?"

"I'm fine, pardner, and I've come out to see you and catch up."

"I've told you what happened to me the night Alonso Alvarado attacked us."

"Yeah, you said you were saved by that dude Tanner that was staying here back then."

"He saved my life, and later I was placed in witness protection."

"That's what you said, but you never told me where they placed you."

"Sorry, Steve, but I was told not to reveal that information to anyone. I've come out of hiding against the better judgement of the U.S. Marshals who run the program."

Mendez smiled at Cody. "I have trouble imagining you hiding from anyone. Pardner, you were always a badass."

Cody grinned. "Look who's talking. Was there anyone at school that you didn't get in a fight with?"

"A few of the teachers, and you—hell, we always got along."

"How long have you been the police chief, Steve?"

"I took the position just twelve weeks ago. Before that, I was with the DEA."

"Why the change?"

"My wife was tired of me being away from home so much, Cody, and she wanted to settle down back home."

"Back home? Do I know her?"

"Hell yeah you know her, I married Ginny Roberts."

"Ginny? You and Ginny are married?"

"That's right, it's been nine years now, and we've got a boy too."

"How is she? I always liked Ginny."

"She liked you too. Remember how she clung to you when we were kids?"

"Yeah, but that changed in high school when she met Roger Delray."

"She and Roger broke up in college, then she married some guy who cheated on her. After she divorced his sorry ass, we ran into each other in Dallas and have been together ever since. Ginny is looking forward to seeing you again."

"Bring her by anytime, Steve."

"We'll make a point of it."

"I guess there aren't too many people from our high school days still in town, hmm?"

"No, everybody that grows up here wanders off to the cities eventually, but guys like us come back. It's because we have the land. It's tough to give up the land, good times or bad."

"It's one of the reasons I'm back. This has been Parker land too long to let it go, and someday, maybe I'll have children to pass it on to."

"That Sara's a looker, Cody, and you always did like the dark-haired beauties. Hey, remember that girl Raven? She was the girlfriend of the quarterback, Jimmy Kyle, now there was a honey." Mendez recalled something and laughed. "Of course, you remember her, you stole her away from Jimmy, didn't you?"

"I did, but he never knew about it. She would visit me here in secret."

"Serves him right, the jerk."

"Is Raven still in town?"

"With her looks, hell no, the story I heard is that she went off to Vegas to be a showgirl."

"She probably made it; she was smart too."

Mendez laughed. "Hey, Cody, remember when Jimmy sicced those friends of his from the football team on us? He caught you and Raven talking in the school parking lot."

Cody nodded, as the memory returned. "It was us against four, and we won."

"I busted a knuckle on one of those kids' teeth and we were all suspended for three days."

"It seemed like you were always being suspended for fighting."

"I was a hothead back then, but I've calmed down over the years."

"I haven't seen Jimmy yet; I wonder if he's changed."

"He hasn't changed. The man is an ass; he's also the mayor."

"I know. I read that in the newspaper. It figures he would grow up to be a politician."

"Mayor Kyle still doesn't like me, not that I give a damn," Mendez said, as Cody's phone vibrated in his pocket.

Cody took out the phone and saw that there were two new visitors. He froze the video that had captured them, then he turned the phone around for Steve to look at, as he asked a question.

"Is that who I think it is?"

"Speak of the devil, yep, that's Jimmy Kyle, and that sourpuss seated beside him is a councilwoman named Gail Avery. She's the mayor's shadow and backs him in all of his boneheaded proposals."

"They're lovers?"

Mendez laughed again. "I'm sure that spinster would

love it if Jimmy jumped her bones, but no, I think she lives in hope; Jimmy still attracts the babes."

Mayor Jimmy Kyle stepped out of his Mercedes and stared over at Cody. Kyle was blond, blue-eyed, and still had the quarterback physique he had when he led the Stark football team.

Gail Avery was looking at Cody as well, and Cody faintly remembered seeing her around town when they were all younger. He guessed that Gail Avery was several years older than the rest of them were. Avery was looking at Cody as if he were a weed she'd found in her garden.

Jimmy Kyle walked over while shaking his head. "I heard you were back from the dead, Cody. It's getting so you can't rely on anything anymore. You know, my granddaddy died that same year; I sure wish he had come back instead of you."

"It's good to see you again too, Jimmy," Cody said.

"I'm the mayor now, did you know that?"

"I did."

"Yeah, we Kyles were born to lead, just like I led the football team back in the old days."

"You guys had a losing record every year if I recall right," Cody said, and some of the starch went out of the mayor.

"I remember you," Gail Avery said. She had a way of speaking that made everything she said sound like an allegation.

Cody tipped the cowboy hat he was wearing at the woman as a way of greeting. The gesture had come naturally and was one he had done many times as a teen and child. He might have been Tanner for nearly twenty years, but he was Cody Parker, Texan, for life.

Avery pointed at Steve Mendez. "You and this one got into all kinds of trouble as kids."

"I suppose we did," Cody said.

"Why are you and Miss Sunshine here, Jimmy?" Mendez asked.

"I wanted to see Cody with my own eyes."

"You've done it, now hit the road."

"You don't tell me when to come and go, Chief. I'm the mayor."

"Cody and I were catching up on old times, and I seem to recall a time or two when I kicked your sorry ass."

Mayor Kyle took a step backwards. "Are you threatening me?"

Mendez smiled. "Just recalling fond memories, but like you said, you're the mayor; you must have important things to do."

"I do at that," Kyle said. He walked back to his car with Avery following. As he opened the door, he looked back at Cody. "Hey, Parker!"

"Yes, Mr. Mayor?"

"I know about you and Raven, and I'll get you back for that someday, yes sir, I will."

After making that pledge, Kyle got in his car and drove off.

"I don't like that threat he made, Cody. The dude is a wimp, but he's a wimp with money and a wee bit of power by being mayor."

"I've been threatened by better," Cody said.

"I've got your back, you know that, right?"

Cody stared at the man who had been a big part of his earlier life. He realized that it pleased him to have a chance to get to know Steve Mendez again.

"I do know that, and I'm glad you stopped by, Steve."

"Same here, pardner. You know, you're the reason I'm a cop."

"I am?"

Mendez made a wide gesture with one arm, indicating the ranch. "The shit that went down here when those cartel members killed your family... it changed me. I had lost my best friend, Cody. You were gone, man, you, your family, just wiped out, and the bastards that did it went back to where they came from and would never be caught." Mendez's face twisted into a grimace of fury. "I can't tell you how angry that made me. After college, I joined the DEA to do something about it."

"Maybe I should have gotten word to you, to tell you I was alive."

"No, you were right to play dead... the thing is, have you risked yourself by coming back?"

"There's a slim chance that I might be attacked here."

"Who would do it? I understood that the man who was behind the massacre is dead."

"That's true, but he discovered I was alive shortly before his death and he became obsessed by the idea of killing me. There's a rumor that he placed a large contract out on me, one that's still open and available to be claimed."

"So, someone might come here and try to harm you?"

"I'll be ready for them. I'm not a boy anymore, and no one will ever hurt my family again."

Mendez nodded. "I bet that's right. Anyway, I'd best be going. There's a man I need to see concerning a murder investigation."

"Are you talking about the Harvey brothers?"

"Yeah, how did you know?"

"I read about their deaths. And remember, I passed through here a few years ago. That was when I met Rich and Ernie. They were hiring themselves out as troublemakers to harass Maria Reyes, the woman I bought the ranch from."

"They were some low-level drug dealers too. I'm guessing they were killed to get them out of the way. If so, it means some serious players are looking to move in."

"What do you plan to do about that?"

"I'll stop it, Cody. This town won't go to hell, not while I'm chief."

"Be careful, Steve."

"I always am. Tell Sara and that little brother of yours I said hi."

"I'll pass it on, but Caleb had to fly back to California for a few days."

"Hearing about what happened to your mother also blew my mind. I'll say this for you, Cody, you don't live a boring life."

"True, but I'm working on it."

Mendez laughed, climbed into his SUV, and drove off.

5

HERE'S TO SECOND CHANCES

SEATTLE, WASHINGTON

DWIGHT PARKED THE MOTORCYCLE IN THE DRIVEWAY OF the Magic Man's suburban home and walked around to the back yard. It was nearly noon and he was at the house for lunch. As usual in the spring, Dr. Baxter was tending to his flower garden. The Magic Man had a green thumb when it came to plants. His yard was filled with black-eyed Susans, cornflowers, geraniums, roses, and other plants. The space was an oasis of beauty and tranquility and had a seven-foot-high privacy fence around it. A stone fountain produced a background sound of trickling water and the flowers gave off a pleasant scent.

When he spotted Dwight, Baxter smiled at him. "We've got a new target."

Dwight grabbed a beer from a foam cooler that was sitting by a gas grill. When Baxter was through with his plants, he would grill hamburgers for the two of them.

After settling into one of a set of white wrought iron chairs with a cushioned seat, Dwight asked a question.

"Who's the new target, anyone interesting?"

"Oh yes, his name is Tanner, and he operates out of New York City."

"Tanner?" Dwight said. "I've heard the name mentioned, but I don't remember who he is."

"The man is an assassin, and it's claimed that he's the best."

Dwight had been slouching, he sat up straight. "Right, Tanner. That's the dude that went down to Mexico and killed that cartel leader a few years ago. Damn, he won't be an easy hit, and he's got a mean rep too."

Baxter took a seat opposite Dwight and took off his gardening gloves. "He'll die as easily as anyone once I ascertain how he thinks. From what I've been told by the client, a Mr. Harkness, Tanner is protecting a man whom Harkness wants to harm. Before he can reach that man, Tanner must be eliminated."

"Tanner is protecting someone? I thought he only killed people?"

"I guess the man can do both."

"Whoever kills Tanner will be famous in some circles."

"Yes, he's the most noteworthy target we've had so far. Given that, I'll be extra cautious in how I go about things."

"What's that mean?"

"It means I'll send problems his way and see how he solves them."

"What sort of problems?"

"His fellow assassins. If he's as good at surviving as I've been led to believe, each time they fail, I'll learn more about Tanner. If they succeed, so much the better."

Dwight drained the beer bottle, then sent Baxter a perplexed look. "How are you going to learn anything if

Tanner kills the guys you send after him? They won't be talking."

"I'm going to send you to New York City to oversee the operation and have the men stay in contact with you by phone."

"Great. I love New York. It will be like a mini vacation."

Baxter left the yard and went into the house. When he returned, he had a plate of hamburger patties, buns, and a bowl of salad.

Dwight plucked a piece of cucumber out of the salad. After chewing it, he asked a question that Baxter hadn't considered.

"What if none of the assassins you send at Tanner can kill him?"

"Excuse me?"

"This Tanner, people have tried to kill him before; they're always the ones who wind up dead. If our guys can't kill him, he may show up here someday looking for you."

Baxter laughed. "You forget that those other people weren't me. Tanner may be a fine marksman and have a talent for survival, but I doubt his intellect is any match for mine. He won't be defeated by might alone, he'll be outmaneuvered by my intelligence. Don't worry, Dwight, the man is as good as dead."

~

STARK, TEXAS, THE PARKER RANCH

THE VETERINARIAN, DR. BETH ALEXANDER WAS AN energetic blonde in her thirties. Sara stood by looking worried as she watched the doctor examine her horse, a mare named Misty.

"Your ranch hand was smart to feed her a little fresh grass, Mrs. Parker. Misty will be fine by tomorrow. It's a mild case of colic."

Sara was pleased by hearing herself referred to as Mrs. Parker, although it was premature. The wedding was still days away.

"Thank you for coming by, Dr. Alexander. I'm glad to hear there's nothing seriously wrong with my horse."

The doctor tilted her head. "You're not from Texas, are you?"

"I grew up in Connecticut then moved to New York City."

"I've never been to either one. I was born in Stark, then moved to Houston as a girl."

"Do you have time for a cup of coffee, Doctor?"

"That sounds nice, and call me—"

"Beth? Is that really you?"

Those words came from Doc. He stood in the doorway of the stable with an expression of shock on his face. When Sara looked back at the doctor, she saw that the woman was equally surprised.

"Daddy?"

Doc moved toward Dr. Alexander as a grin brightened his face. The smile disappeared when Dr. Alexander admonished him to stay back.

"Stop right there. I want nothing to do with you."

"Honey... I... I know I was never there for you, and I apologize for that, Beth, but I've stopped drinking, I have."

Dr. Alexander shook her head. "You told me the same thing years ago, and then you showed up drunk at my graduation ceremony."

Doc moaned at the memory. "I know, and honey, that

was one of the things that made me stop drinking for good." Doc pulled a bronzed sobriety chip out of his side pocket. The chip signified that he'd been sober for ten years. "See, I really have stopped drinking. And honey, I've missed you so much."

Dr. Alexander stared at the chip, then shook her head. "For all I know you bought that on the internet."

Sara spoke up. "For what it's worth, Doctor, I've never seen your father drink, and he takes care of this ranch whenever we're away. We trust him."

Dr. Alexander grabbed her equipment case from where it sat on the ground in front of the stall. It was a blue cloth bag with many compartments and had a strap to make it easy to shoulder carry.

"I gave my father opportunities to reconnect with me when I was younger, too many chances. It was nice meeting you, Mrs. Parker."

As she moved past him, Doc raised a hand as if he were going to grab his daughter's arm. He decided against it, and let his hand drop to his side.

Sara went to him. "Are you all right?"

Doc looked up at her with wet eyes. "My little girl hates me, Sara."

"Did you know her last name was Alexander?"

"The last time I saw Beth, I... I was an embarrassment to her in front of her friends. She told me then that she never wanted to see me again. I didn't blame her for feeling like that, and I stayed away. I guess she married some guy named Alexander." Doc's mood brightened as he realized something. "She's a doctor too."

"In a way she followed in your footsteps."

"I'm sure it wasn't to be like me. I fell into the bottle when Beth was just a little thing; I was a horrible father."

"Maybe, but that's in the past. Now you have a second chance to get to know her."

"I don't think so. Beth still doesn't want me in her life."

"She may in time, Doc, and now you're living in the same town again."

"That was part of the reason I wanted to settle down in Stark. I was hoping I might see Beth again someday. After I sobered up, I looked for her in Houston but couldn't find her."

Sara patted him on the arm. "Give it time, Doc."

"Yeah," Doc said. "Maybe someday she'll give me another chance… not that I deserve it."

Doc left the stable with his sobriety chip clutched tightly in his hand.

6

A CLOSE CALL

BAHIA MAR, CALIFORNIA

THIS IS STUPID, CALEB, STUPID, STUPID, STUPID, CALEB told himself as he gave Dr. Jennifer Mao a ride to her mother's home. It was bad enough that the doctor had run into him on the flight to California and could easily lead the cops to discover his real name, now she also knew what he drove.

"Do I have to keep calling you Stark, or can I learn your real name?" Jen asked.

Caleb sighed in surrender. Why not give her his name? If she was going to tell the police about him, they already knew enough to track him down.

"My name is Caleb."

"Caleb? I like that name; it's sort of old-fashioned."

"Can I call you Jen?"

She reached out and touched the back of Caleb's hand. "You saved my life the other day. You can call me anything you'd like."

"I hope that gratitude means you're not going to talk to the cops or the Feds about me."

"I had my chance to do that when Agent Eriksen told me about you in the hospital."

"True, but that was before you knew my real name."

"What's your last name, Caleb?"

"It's Knox, well actually Parker, but I still go by Knox."

"You have two last names? And I guess it's three if you count the name Stark."

"It's a long story."

"That's okay; you can tell it to me when we go out on our date."

Caleb turned his head and grinned at her. "We're going on a date?"

"It's up to you, but I'd like to know you better."

"Same here," Caleb said.

Jen told him to turn left at the next traffic light, which they caught red. As they sat at the light, Caleb asked Jen about her mother and sister.

"My sister and mom visited me in the hospital in Texas but they both had to get back to work. While I'm here, I'm going to look for a house, something small. I still have to sell the home I have in Texas."

"As a doctor, I guess you won't have a problem finding work."

"No, I shouldn't. Unfortunately, there's always a need for emergency medicine."

"Your skill is the reason why you were kidnapped."

"Yes, and if those men had taken their friend to a hospital like I told them to, the man would still be alive."

"I'm sure you did what you could for him."

"I did, but he had lost too much blood."

They reached Jen's home and Caleb pulled in front of the driveway. The well-cared for colonial-style home was two-stories high and had a green manicured lawn out front.

"Why don't you come in? My mother will be home soon. She'd love to meet the man who saved me from that fire."

"That's not a good idea; it's bad enough that you know who I am."

"You're right. I'm sorry. I'm not used to dealing with secrets like yours, but I'll never tell anyone about you, I swear, Caleb."

He grinned again. "So, when are we going on this date?"

"I'll give you my phone number and we'll talk."

Caleb exchanged cell phone numbers with Jen. When he looked up from inputting the number, in the rearview mirror he saw a Black SUV pulling to the curb two car lengths behind him. When he realized who the driver was, his shoulders slumped as his heart sped up.

"I should have known I was being played."

"What are you talking about?" Jen asked.

Caleb tossed a thumb over his shoulder. "She's here; you don't need to pretend anymore."

"Who's here?" Jen said. When she looked out the pickup truck's rear window, she saw Agent Eriksen getting out of the SUV.

"Oh my God, Caleb, you have to get out of here."

"You two weren't working together to trap me?"

"No, I told you I won't burn you like that. Now get out of here while I see what she wants."

Caleb leaned over and kissed Jen on the cheek. "I look forward to our date."

"Me too," Jen said, as she opened the passenger door to leave.

~

Eriksen watched Jen exit Caleb's truck in a rush while grabbing a suitcase, then she saw the guilty grin on the doctor's face. Jen Mao looked like a kid who'd been caught with their hand in the cookie jar.

"Hello, Doctor, I see you were dropped off by a friend."

"Yes, hi Agent Eriksen—what are you doing here?"

Eriksen squinted at Caleb's departing pickup truck, but she was too far away to make out the license plate number.

"Agent Eriksen?"

"I spoke to your mother by phone the other day and she informed me that you would be in the state for a visit. I wanted to do a follow-up interview with you regarding your abduction. There's still some confusion over where Roy Wicks might have obtained a supply of dynamite."

"Oh, okay. Let's go inside where we can get comfortable."

"The young man who dropped you off wasn't very chivalrous was he?"

"What do you mean?"

Eriksen pointed at Jen's suitcase. "He could have stayed and helped you carry your bag inside."

"There was no need. It's not heavy and it rolls on wheels."

"I see."

Jen tensed up visibly. Eriksen assumed she was expecting her to ask more questions about her friend in the truck. Instead, the FBI agent smiled and made a request.

"If it's not too much trouble, can I have a cup of coffee once we get inside?"

"Sure, yes, and I'll just be a moment while I put my bag in my old bedroom."

"Are you thinking of moving back here?"

"Texas was nice, but now that my sister is no longer going to school there, I might as well move back home. For now, I'll be going back and forth."

"My husband is from Chicago, and he's moving here too, thank God. It was difficult maintaining a long-distance relationship."

"I can imagine. Is he a government agent too?"

"No, John is a businessman."

Jen opened the front door of the home and was greeted by a Siamese cat. After leading Eriksen into the living room, Jen told the agent she would be back in a few moments.

"Then we'll go into the kitchen and talk over coffee."

"I look forward to it," Eriksen said.

Once she was alone, Eriksen took out her phone and called her superior.

"Hi, Candance. I've reconsidered taking some time off as you suggested, if that's still all right?"

"All right? Amanda, you survived a helicopter crash and an explosion. Take a week off."

"Three days should be enough," Eriksen said.

She was betting that Dr. Jennifer Mao would lead her to the mysterious man in the truck within that timeframe. If her instincts were right, she was on the verge of finding Stark.

7

LOOKING FOR MR. TANNER

MANHATTAN

INSIDE A CONFERENCE ROOM ON THE TWENTY-EIGHTH floor of an office building, three members of Blue Truth were meeting to discuss Tanner.

Victor Middleton was leading the discussion. He was a tall man, graying, and an ex-homicide detective from Philadelphia. Sofia Diaz was a squat woman in her forties with long ebony hair, large hazel eyes, and a keen intellect. The former district attorney from New Mexico was excited to be a part of the team chosen to look into the myth of Tanner. She loved solving puzzles and found the case intriguing.

The third member of the group was a black man named Derek Warner. The ex-FBI agent was powerfully-built and had a shaved head.

Victor was handing out interview assignments. "We received an email back from Sara Blake. Sofia, you'll be meeting with her at a hotel coffee shop in Midtown this week."

"I know Blake by reputation," Derek Warner said. "She was obsessed with finding Tanner at one time and claimed to have done so in Las Vegas years ago."

"That's right," Victor said. "She left the Bureau under a cloud. The rumor was that she shot her own partner."

"That's what I heard too," Derek said. "If so, she was never charged."

"An interesting woman," Sofia said. "She may lead us right to the truth about Tanner."

"Who am I interviewing?" Derek asked.

"You're going to like this. I want you to talk to Joe Pullo."

"The mob boss?"

"I've been told it's common knowledge on the street that Joe Pullo and Tanner are good friends."

"Good friends?" Sofia said.

"That's what they're saying, of course, 'they' also say that Tanner went down to Mexico and killed the cartel leader Alonso Alvarado by himself. And oh yeah, Tanner singlehandedly defeated the Conglomerate and that bunch of scum bags who were calling themselves the Brotherhood."

Derek grinned. "If Tanner's not a myth, then he's a cross between Superman and Batman."

Victor nodded. "I know, it sounds like he must be a myth. Then again, someone using the name of Tanner has been active in New York over the last several years, then there was that flyer being passed around at one time."

"I saw that flyer," Derek said. "The eyes on the dude in the picture made him look like a demon or something. I know we need to keep an open mind, but I think Tanner is just a phantom."

"He's a phantom with a very long life," Sofia countered. "An assassin going by the name of Tanner has been said to have been around for over a hundred years. He first appeared in Chicago back before Prohibition, there have also been reports from Detroit, Louisiana, the southwest, Las Vegas, and even Europe and Australia, and don't forget that file we were given and the conversation it contained."

Sofia was referring to an interview conducted by the initial team of Blue Truth personnel responsible for evaluating the possible legitimacy of myths or legends to investigate. The file held a conversation one of the investigators had with a man named Christopher Allen. Allen claimed that in 1966 he had trained as an apprentice assassin with a man identifying himself as Tanner Four.

Allen asserted that he was disqualified when he failed an endurance test in the desert. He also said that a man named Farnsworth was eventually named Tanner Five.

"I read that interview," Derek said. "It stated in the closing paragraph that Mr. Allen was seventy-eight and suffering from dementia. It's possible the man made the entire story up from something half-remembered."

"I don't know, Derek," Victor said. "The claim that one Tanner passes on the title to a successor sounds likely to me. It would also explain why the current Tanner is so formidable. He would have the advantage of possessing the knowledge, experience, and skills of the six men who came before him."

"I still think it sounds unlikely. These are thugs we're talking about, hit men, the scum of the earth. Men like that don't know a damn thing about honor and tradition."

Sofia wagged a finger at Derek. "You said the same thing when we were considering looking into the legend of the Scallato clan in Sicily, and remember, that turned out to be true."

"That's debatable, and yeah, I read that book written by Jacques Durand, but I'm still not convinced."

"Why not? Durand made a strong case for Maurice Scallato having been the last of a long line of assassins."

"I know, but he also insinuated in the book that it was Tanner who killed Scallato, in a sort of hit man versus hit man battle to the death."

"He never said it was Tanner," Sofia said. "He called the man Banner."

"Yeah, but he described him as having intense eyes, just like everyone says Tanner has."

"Maybe we should interview Durand, Victor," Sofia said. "I volunteer to travel to France."

"If that becomes necessary, I'll be the one taking that pleasure trip. Instead, I'm heading down to Arkansas for my interview."

"Who are you seeing?" Derek said.

"I'll be meeting two men who once claimed to have captured Tanner. They made statements to the Nevada police about it at the time."

"That sounds promising too," Sofia said. "What are the men's names?"

"They're brothers," Victor said. "Merle and Earl Carter."

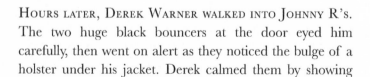

HOURS LATER, DEREK WARNER WALKED INTO JOHNNY R'S. The two huge black bouncers at the door eyed him carefully, then went on alert as they noticed the bulge of a holster under his jacket. Derek calmed them by showing his FBI credentials. The word, RETIRED, was stamped across it.

"I'd like to see Joe Pullo. I called ahead and he agreed to speak with me."

One of the bouncers told Derek to follow him and led the way over to a private elevator. After a ride up one level, Derek was escorted into Pullo's plush office. The office was soundproof and blocked out the loud music of the club. Still, there was the sense of a slight vibration emanating from the floor. Pullo could activate speakers if he wished to hear what was going on below while a wall of one-way mirrors offered a grand view of the stages. The two women wowing the crowd made Derek wish he were single again, and younger.

Pullo was alone in the office, when he offered Derek a drink, Derek thanked him and said he'd have a beer.

"I watch that TV show you guys have, Blue Truth Investigates, that episode you did on that wack job The King of Killers was my favorite."

"You probably don't remember but we met once, Pullo."

Joe stared at him, then snapped his fingers. "Brooklyn, six years ago, you were investigating a heist of some electronic equipment from a warehouse on the docks."

"You have a good memory."

"No better than yours."

"I don't know, I didn't go on in life to head a crime family, that makes you memorable."

Pullo looked at Derek with a guileless expression. "Crime family? I manage this bar and a few other enterprises. I don't know anything about a crime family."

"Right, and I suppose you don't know anything about a hit man named Tanner either, do you?"

A smile spread over Joe's face, then morphed into a chuckle. "You guys are chasing after Tanner?"

Derek frowned at Pullo. He wasn't a believer in Tanner. That didn't mean he didn't take his job seriously.

"That's right. Why is that so funny? Are you saying he doesn't exist?"

"Oh, Tanner is real, real old that is, he's been bumping off guys for over a hundred years."

"We've heard those stories too. It's possible that the name has been handed down from one man to the next."

"Yeah, it's been handed down, but like a compliment, you know? Like if a guy is smart you call him an Einstein, or if he's a magician you nickname him Houdini. There probably was a real guy named Tanner back when the myth first started, but now it's just a nickname a guy gets put on him. It means he's a great assassin."

"You learned all that managing a strip club?"

Pullo shrugged. "You hear things at the bar."

As DEREK WAS WALKING BACK THROUGH THE CLUB, HE tore his eyes away from the stage long enough to look around. That's when he spotted Tamir Ivanov working as a bartender. Ivanov was the man who actually ran Johnny R's, and was just helping out at the bar during a rush. Like Derek, he was ex-FBI. After leaving the elevator, Derek headed over to talk to him.

"Tamir, you work here?"

Ivanov blinked in surprise at seeing Derek as he filled a pitcher with beer. "Hello, Derek. Yeah, I tend bar here sometime, you know, to supplement the retirement."

"In a place like this?"

Ivanov nodded at the stage, where nineteen-year-old redheaded twins were displaying how flexible they both were. "It has its perks."

The two talked about old times for a few minutes before Derek left the club. Ivanov departed the bar and went upstairs to speak to Pullo. Pullo greeted Ivanov by calling him by his nickname.

"What's up, Fed?"

"I see Derek Warner was here. He's former FBI, but he told me he was working with Blue Truth now."

"Yeah, they're looking into Tanner. Get this, they want to find out if he's real. I told Warner that Tanner was just a name some hitters used."

"I once thought he was a myth, and I doubt Derek believes the stories either. There's just one thing."

"What's that?"

"Derek Warner, when he left the Bureau it wasn't under the best of circumstances. Nothing official was ever put in his record, but he was suspected by some of killing drug dealers."

"To rob them?"

Ivanov shook his head. "No robberies, just murder. It's not widely known, but there's been a suspicion for years that there's a subculture throughout law enforcement that acts as vigilantes."

"And you think Derek Warner might be one of them?"

Ivanov sighed. "I'm hardly one to throw stones, given what I did to Michael Krupin as payback for his killing my partner, but yes. Derek may say he's looking for Tanner to arrest him; then again, he may be part of a group that wants him dead."

Joe nodded. "Thanks, Fed, I'll let Tanner know that the stakes might be higher than he thinks."

"Yeah, he might want to keep his head down for a while."

Pullo laughed. "I've known Tanner for fifteen years. He ain't the shy retiring type."

Ivanov left the office to return downstairs, and Joe removed a phone from a drawer to call Tanner.

8

CHANGES

THE PARKER RANCH, STARK, TEXAS, THE
FOLLOWING MORNING

CODY AND SARA HAD MADE A NUMBER OF CHANGES TO THE
ranch since taking possession of it. This included the
addition of a landing strip for private airplanes. As for the
plane, Cody had yet to buy it; however, a large hangar had
been built near the landing strip to house one.

Cody sat in a Jeep with its top off as he watched a
Cessna 400 come in for a landing. Seated beside Cody was
Romeo, whom he had picked up from the airport earlier
that morning. Although the wedding was less than a week
away, Romeo had come alone, with Nadya and Florentina
to follow in a few days' time. Nadya thought it best not to
have an energetic toddler like Florentina underfoot while
Sara was preparing the ranch for a wedding.

The pilot of the Cessna was Spenser Hawke. After he
landed smoothly, Cody drove the Jeep over to the plane.

Spenser was smiling, but Cody could tell straight

away that something was bothering his mentor. When he realized that Spenser had arrived alone, he asked about it.

"Where's Amy? Is she arriving later in the week?"

The smile left Spenser's face and a sadness entered his eyes. "I didn't want to mention this right away, but I should have known you'd find her absence odd. Amy and I are no longer together, Cody. The truth is, she left me."

AFTER SECURING THE PLANE IN THE HANGAR, SPENSER revealed that Amy, a former Hollywood makeup artist, was asked by an old friend to work on her newest film. The friend had grown successful and was directing a movie with a huge special effects budget. Amy agreed to join the production, while telling Spenser that it would only be for a few weeks. Delays on the sets stretched the weeks into months. Along with that, Amy was working with a man who had been her first love.

He was a special effects supervisor and was recently divorced. Old passions reunited when the two began working closely together on the film, and Amy admitted to Spenser that she had cheated on him.

"I was willing to forgive her; after all, I'm no saint either... that's when Amy told me that she'd been having second thoughts about us for a while."

"Nadya wondered about that, since you and Amy had been engaged for so long," Romeo said.

Spenser nodded. "That was Amy; whenever I asked her to set a date for the wedding, she delayed doing so."

"Amy is staying in California?" Cody asked.

"She got back together with her first love and plans to keep working in Hollywood."

Cody gripped his mentor's shoulder. "I'm sorry, Spenser. I know you loved her."

"I still do, but that's enough about me, Mr. Parker."

"That's right, I'm Cody Parker again, and if I want to make this work, I'll need you and Romeo to help me."

"You said that when we talked on the phone. You also said you wanted to discuss the Tanner legacy."

"Yeah, Spenser. I want to make changes, big changes, but I wanted to talk it over with you and Romeo first."

"With me?" Romeo said.

"You trained to be a Tanner, and you even carried out a contract as one once, shortly after Spenser lost his eye."

"I did fill in for him, but that didn't make me a Tanner."

Cody smiled at him. "That's one of the things I want to change."

Spenser cocked his head, as Cody's words intrigued him. "I can't wait to hear what you have in mind."

Sara had given Spenser a hug of sympathy when she learned of his and Amy's breakup, and was surprised by it.

"I know she loved you."

"She did, just not enough," Spenser said.

After discussing the upcoming wedding and the excitement of moving to the ranch, Cody, Romeo, and Spenser had retired into the office to talk. Sara told Cody that she had an errand to run and left the house, while Doc was out on a riding mower cutting the grass. The sound of the mower's engine could be heard rising and falling as Doc created neat rows of freshly mowed lawn.

Spenser and Romeo sat to Cody's right on a brown leather sofa. Cody was settled into a matching wing chair, and a carafe of coffee was on a low pine table along with fresh blueberry muffins that Sara had baked.

"The world is changing," Cody said, "and we have to change with it."

"In what ways?" Spenser asked.

"A Tanner has always been a sort of jack of all trades, while mastering some. That was fine when the world was less complicated, but it takes a specialist to do most things well or exceptionally. A Tanner needs to specialize in weapons, physical combat, and other ways to kill. Tracking down targets and acquiring contracts could better be handled by someone else, so could the research that's sometimes required."

"I agree," Spenser said. "The problem has always been in finding the right people, especially when it comes to working with a go-between to handle clients. Ideally, we should never meet a client, or even know their name."

"I wouldn't want to be excluded from the vetting process completely, but yeah, intermediaries have always been a problem. Like you, Spenser, I've gone through a few of them for one reason or another."

"That was why when I first met you here in Stark, I was coming to see the client myself. The go-between I'd been using had been arrested for driving drunk. I figured the man was unreliable and stopped using him."

"I want to change that by hiring someone to be a permanent intermediary. I don't have anyone in mind yet but there must be someone out there who would be perfect for the job. As for a researcher, I've already put one on retainer."

Spenser looked surprised by that. "There's someone you trust enough to let them know your target's name?"

"I'm using Zoe Farnsworth, Tanner Five's granddaughter. The woman is a hacker and she works fast.

Since she's already connected to us, I don't need to worry that she'll be a problem down the line."

"How is Zoe doing, Cody?" Romeo asked. He and Zoe had been lovers when they were younger.

"She and Kayla are both great, and they're still working as bounty hunters, so I might also use their tracking skills from time to time."

"That idea about finding a dedicated go-between is great," Romeo said. "My biggest problem is finding new clients, and I take only three or four contracts a year these days."

"I may have more work for you someday soon if you want it. Once I find a reliable mediator, you'll have access to them too."

"It's a great idea, Cody," Spenser said. "But where are you going to find someone like you describe?"

"Maybe I'll get them from the ranks of Ordnance Inc."

"Ordnance Inc.? Isn't that the group that tried to kill you?"

"They are, and they'll try again someday, I don't doubt it at all. When they come, I'll be ready for them… and I want your help."

"You've got it," Romeo and Spenser said at the same time.

"Ordnance Inc. is a massive association of mercenaries who have united to form an organization. They have no problem getting clients, and that means there's someone within the group who handles that."

"True," Spenser said. "But remember, they'll work for anyone and do anything that's asked of them. As a Tanner, your client list and the targets you'll take on are more selective."

"I know, but I still think we can adapt their model and make it our own."

"Once we destroy them?"

"Which we will."

"What if they don't break the truce you have with them, bro?" Romeo asked.

"Then I'd have to find another way, but Ordnance Inc. will attack me someday. I recently had a conversation with the man who runs it, Trevor Healy. He no longer fears me, and he believes he has enough people to kill me. They'll make a play; the question is when."

"Are you prepared for an all-out attack by superior forces?" Spenser asked, while looking around.

"We are. Sara and I spent the last few months getting the ranch ready. I'll show you what we did after this meeting."

"What were these plans you had for me, Cody?" Romeo asked. "Were you talking about helping you with Ordnance Inc.?"

"Not just that, no, I want to make a fundamental change to the way Tanners are chosen, and the way we operate."

Spenser sat up straighter. "What sort of changes?"

"Think back to when Farnsworth passed the Tanner name on to you, what was that like?"

Spenser grinned. "It was one of the proudest moments of my life."

"Yes, and mine too, but although I had been named a Tanner and was the latest in a line of men who'd had the name, I was still starting from scratch."

Spenser nodded in understanding. "Yes, I remember that feeling too. Farnsworth had been Tanner for decades, but that did me no good. I still had to prove myself and find my own clients."

"Right," Cody said. "But that's making it harder than it has to be. Wouldn't it be better to hand over the title while also supplying a way to find clients, and have an experienced support staff? The way technology is changing everything, and with cameras popping up everywhere, it's more difficult than ever to keep from being filmed or tracked. In another few years, it may become next to impossible."

"There are ways around that, like a hacker could go into the digital files and erase your tracks and images," Spenser said.

"That's a possibility, but it could take too long to make it workable. I've come up with another idea, one that will also convince this group Blue Truth that Tanner is just the legend that most cops suspect him to be."

"How's all this involve me?" Romeo said.

Cody smiled. "I want you to be Tanner Eight."

"What? Dude, you're retiring?"

"I'm not retiring, not anytime soon."

"Then I don't get it."

"My brother, Caleb, he asked me last week why you weren't named Tanner Eight when I was named Tanner Seven. I realized then that the only answer I had for him was that choosing one Tanner at a time was the way we'd always done things. It struck me then that there was no real reason why there couldn't be two Tanners, or even three. You were good enough to be a Tanner, Romeo, and you still are."

Spenser stood and began pacing with a thoughtful expression darkening his face. "I understand what you're saying, but I don't think it would work."

"What's your objection?" Cody asked.

"Human nature. While it's true that you and Romeo could make it work, you two are the exception. From day one I was amazed at how well you got along with each other. And that was despite being rivals for a position only one of you could have someday. I don't think that would be common. Look at the nightmare that happened because Farnsworth had to train me to replace Vince Ryker. Ryker refused to accept me as a Tanner and considered himself one until the day he died. We don't need a repeat of that."

Cody hung his head. "Damn it, you're right. I was considering this based on Romeo and me. That said, I would still like to offer Romeo the title of Tanner Eight. He deserves it."

Romeo leaned over and punched Cody on the shoulder. "Dude, that offer is unbelievable."

"Do you accept?"

"No, Cody. I'll have to say no."

"Why?"

"Cody, I'm in great shape, I'm about as deadly as they come, and I make it a point to learn new skills every year, but... I'm not in your league. You're phenomenal, dude, and I'll have your back, but you're Tanner."

"You're good enough to be a Tanner, Romeo."

"I was, at one time, but not now."

"I don't understand what you mean."

Romeo was about to say something, then glanced at Spenser and remained silent.

Spenser smiled. "He's trying not to hurt my feelings, Cody, but Romeo was right when he called you phenomenal. You are without a doubt the deadliest man alive and you've been forced to prove it again and again. I was great, all of the previous Tanners were great, but Cody, you're one of a kind."

"I am what I am because of you."

"In part, yes, but you surpassed me even before you were named a Tanner. You've nearly made the name a household word and the legend is ten times greater than it ever was. If it wasn't, an organization like Blue Truth would have no interest in getting to the root of the myth."

"Yes, the name Tanner is feared and respected. That's why I don't want to let what I've worked for just die once the name is passed on to a successor. If the client never meets anyone but the go-between, they'll never be aware if I'm handling the contract or if it's the man who succeeds me someday. I want the transition to be seamless, which will only make the legend and reputation grow as the years pass."

"It's ambitious, especially given the fact that you're under investigation."

"That investigation couldn't have come at a better time; I have a way to turn it into an advantage."

"How?" Romeo asked.

Cody picked up the carafe and poured more coffee into his cup. "My plan involves a man named Duke."

9

SETTING THE TRAP

UPPER MANHATTAN

Duke used a key to open the door on the space he planned to use as a temporary home. It was a loft apartment that overlooked Frederick Douglass Boulevard in Harlem.

After learning that Ordnance Inc. was after him while working for Harkness, Duke and his daughter Lisa had extended their stay at Tanner's penthouse. Once Tanner told him that Ordnance Inc. was no longer a factor, Duke decided to find a new home. He didn't want to impose on Sara and Tanner's generosity anymore than he already had.

The loft had three bedrooms. One would be his, the second Lisa's, while the third could be used as Lisa's workshop. Duke was certain that Harkness wouldn't be able to find them in Harlem, and in the meantime, he could hire someone to track down Harkness. When the window he was standing near shattered from a bullet being fired through it, Duke knew he had underestimated Jared Harkness.

ON A NEARBY ROOFTOP, DWIGHT WAS GRINNING AS HE PUT away his gun. He had almost blown Duke's head off, although he had only been trying to frighten the man. Dwight figured if he were a better shot, he would have missed by a wider margin.

A private investigator working for the Magic Man uncovered an alias of Duke Philips. Someone using that name rented the loft space where Dwight had discovered Duke. The private investigator had also provided a photo of Duke, which was taken from his file in New York State's department of motor vehicles.

The Magic Man had sent Dwight to New York to lure Tanner into showing himself. The best way to do that was to place the life of Tanner's friend in danger. Once Duke told Tanner that Harkness had sent someone else to kill him, the hit man would show himself.

When that happens, Dwight mused, *the real fun will begin.*

The Magic Man had several assassins heading to New York City to test Tanner. They would be sent at the man one after the other and record the events that followed.

Dwight was hoping that they would fail, while at the same time provide enough data for the Magic Man to come up with a plan to deal with Tanner. Dwight wanted to be the one to put the plan into effect. If he were to kill Tanner, his stock in the underworld would go up a hundredfold.

Dwight left the roof and went down to street level. He had orders to follow Duke, so that they'd know where to find him once the first hit man arrived in town. After buying a pretzel from a street vendor, Dwight walked over to the nondescript rental car he had. He kept an eye on the front of the building, since it was the only way for Duke to leave. While it was true that the building the loft was in had a rear door, Dwight had used quick-drying epoxy to weld it shut from the outside.

Twenty-six minutes passed before Duke peeked his head out the front door, Dwight was ducked down in his seat and difficult to see. A moment later, Duke sprinted for his van, got inside, and sped away from the curb.

Dwight let him go. He had slapped a magnetic tracking device onto the underside of Duke's vehicle and could follow him at a distance. Twenty seconds after Duke's departure, Dwight started his engine and followed. Working for the Magic Man was almost as much fun as playing video games.

BACK IN STARK, SARA ENTERED THE OFFICE BELONGING TO the veterinarian Dr. Alexander. She was carrying two coffees she'd bought at the shop across the street.

As the fiancée and future bride of Cody Parker, Sara was a minor celebrity in Stark. People stared and whispered while pointing her out to others. She took it with good humor. Once the town had grown used to the fact that Cody had survived the massacre that wiped out his family, they would be treated like anyone else. She wanted that: to live the quiet life in the country, and she also wanted it for her future children.

The receptionist's desk was empty, as Dr. Alexander had no need for one. She either answered the phone herself or was forwarded messages by a service she used.

Sara called out, "Hello?" and the doctor soon

appeared from behind a curtain. When she saw Sara, a worried look came over her.

"My father asked you to talk to me?"

"No, he doesn't know I'm here. We were about to have coffee yesterday when you left, so I thought I'd bring it to you."

"I was just thinking of taking a break and getting a cup, so thank you."

Dr. Alexander told Sara to follow her into the back room and to have a seat in front of the desk. Instead of settling behind her wooden desk, the doctor sat in the chair that was to the left of Sara.

"I'm Beth by the way, and you're Sara?"

"That's right, and calling me Mrs. Parker was a bit premature. The wedding doesn't take place for another few days."

Beth's mouth opened in surprise. "Oh, you're those Parkers, yes, I've heard about you. It's a remarkable story, what happened to your fiancé, and so tragic."

"It is both of those," Sara agreed.

"My mother had already moved us to Houston when that happened, but we saw it on the news. I remember your fiancé a little, and also his sisters, although they were two or three years behind me in school."

"Cody has come back to Stark to reclaim his heritage, and we'll spend the rest of our lives here."

"I don't have a ranch, but I've always loved this area. Houston moved at a faster pace than I like, and I enjoy caring for horses, and also riding them."

"You have horses of your own?"

"I do, and my home sits on eight acres, so I've a little room for our horses. We're a short ride from your land, just across the old Kinney ranch."

"Cody and I are buying that property."

"To extend your ranch?"

"Yes."

"That will give you plenty of land to ride on."

"Your father likes to ride too, and he's proud of you."

"I always wanted to be a vet, ever since I was a kid, but Sara, I'd rather not talk about my father. I really want nothing to do with him."

"He's stopped drinking, Beth, and he's a good man."

"I don't care. I meant what I said when I told him he was out of chances. I don't want my father in my life again."

A small voice spoke up from the doorway leading to the reception area.

"Father? Mom, your father is alive?"

Beth spilt her coffee onto the front of her smock as she stood. "Kelly, why are you here so early?"

"School was only half a day because the summer break starts soon, remember?"

"Right, I'd forgotten."

Kelly was nine. She sent Sara a smile as she walked over to the desk, where she then stared at her mother.

"I have a grandfather?"

"He's... yes."

"I want to meet him. Who is he?"

"That's not a good idea, Kelly. Your grandfather is not someone I want in our lives."

"But he's your father, Mom."

Sara stood and sent Beth an apologetic smile. She hadn't come there to cause friction between Beth and her daughter. After sighing, Beth introduced her to Kelly.

"You might as well call her Mrs. Parker, since that's who she'll be in a few more days."

"I heard about Cody Parker. Everyone thought he was dead, right?"

Sara smiled at the little girl. "That about sums it up."

As Beth escorted Sara to the door, she asked a favor of her. "Please, don't mention anything about Kelly to my father."

Sara frowned, but she nodded agreement. "I won't say anything. But this is a small town. Doc is bound to find out that you have a daughter."

Beth blinked in surprise. "People still call him Doc?"

"Yes, I didn't know his name was Graham until recently."

"They shouldn't call him that; he hasn't practiced medicine since I was a little girl, when he crawled into a bottle."

"I want you to remember something."

"What's that, Sara?"

"Not only did your father crawl into that bottle, but he made it back out."

Sara left without another word, as behind her, Beth slowly closed the door.

10

TROUBLE IN THE DESERT

THE PARKER RANCH, STARK, TEXAS

Cody, Spenser, and Romeo had moved their conversation out onto the front porch, where the air was filled with the scent of fresh-cut grass.

"Did you say a hundred and eighty million?" Spenser asked Cody.

"That's right. When I was working for the CIA in Europe, I wound up with the fortune in euros that a man named Cal Vernon stole. When converted to dollars, it's around a hundred and eighty million."

"Bro," Romeo said. "That's a helluva lot of cash."

"It is, and it's come in handy. We're using some of it to buy an adjacent ranch that's for sale to extend our land. I'll also be spending a portion of it to fund the Tanner legacy. Future Tanners will train right here on the ranch."

Spenser made a sound of appreciation. "A dedicated space for training will be great, but first you have to find an apprentice."

"I've ideas about that too, but they can wait until after Sara and I are more settled here."

Spenser gazed about. "I know this is a different house, but the ranch has the same feel to it that it did when I first came here. I'm happy that you've come back to reclaim your identity, Cody, but I can't help but feel sadness as well. You don't know how many times I've wished I had done things differently back then... maybe there would have been a better outcome."

"You did everything you could to protect us, Spenser; I'm only alive because of you."

"I still feel like I failed your father. Frank Parker hired me to protect his family, and we all know what happened."

"Spenser," Romeo said. "Both you and Cody need to forgive yourselves. Alonzo Alvarado rolled in here with a small army and caught everyone unaware. If you'd been here, both you and Cody would have died."

"That won't ever happen again," Cody said. "Not with the precautions Sara and I have taken."

"I still don't like the fact that Trevor Healy knows that Tanner is Cody Parker," Spenser said.

"Neither do I, but he's kept it to himself, and I have spies in his organization. When he's ready to make his move, I should get a heads up from one of them."

"There's something else you have to consider. If you were attacked here by a massive force, when it was over, your identity of Cody Parker would be blown."

Cody shook his head. "I've thought of that, Spenser. I've told you about Thomas Lawson and the power he has in the government. He's also no fan of Ordnance Inc. Lawson is ready to pounce on them if they strike. Whatever goes down between Ordnance Inc. and me will be placed under the umbrella called national security and covered up. Lawson will also initiate a cleanup plan to go after the group's minions. If Healy breaks the truce and attacks, he'll be signing Ordnance Inc.'s death warrant."

Spenser patted Cody on the arm. "You've been planning a response for a while, good boy. I'm glad to see you're taking the threat seriously."

"Ordnance Inc. aren't the only ones who have been prepping for war."

Cody's phone made a sound that let him know someone had entered the driveway. It was Sara returning home. She joined the men on the porch and told Cody about her conversation with Beth Alexander.

"Doc has a granddaughter? He'll be thrilled," Cody said.

"Yes, but he'll have to find out on his own."

"That won't take long, not in a town this small. By the way, how do you like Stark so far?"

"It's exactly what I'd thought it would be, quaint and friendly. People are already calling me Mrs. Parker."

"It is a nice town," Cody said, "and I hope it always stays that way."

AT THE STARK POLICE STATION, STEVE MENDEZ WAS meeting with a man inside his office with the door closed. The older gentleman was named Mr. Darby, and he had news for the chief. Colton Darby was a rangy sort with sun-weathered skin and bright blue eyes. He had lived in Stark since he was a boy of three.

Mendez sat behind his desk with his boots up and resting on a corner of it. The black Stetson he liked to wear had been placed on top of a filing cabinet near the door.

"I flew my plane over to Brownsville to visit my sister,"

Darby said. "On the trip back, I spotted something out in the desert that you'd want to know about."

"What would that be, Mr. Darby?"

"Someone erected a shack out there about twelve miles from the highway, you can reach the spot by heading due north past the old Taco Queen. There was smoke coming out of that shack, and three vehicles parked near it. I know from reading the papers that meth dealers like to cook that poison out in the desert, and that's what it made me think of."

"You may be right, and thank you for reporting what you saw. I'll look into it."

Darby stood. He had done what he'd intended, and now it was time to leave. Mendez walked with him to the door, where Darby turned and spoke to him with a serious tone.

"I know you're not new in town, Chief, but you have been gone for a while and living in cities. I hope you don't let any of this drug business get a foothold in Stark. Once that happens, this town will never be the same."

Mendez stared into the old man's eyes. "Mr. Darby, trust me when I tell you that I will see that never happens."

Darby stared back at the chief and was satisfied at what he saw in the man's gaze.

"All right then, but now tell me something else. What's Cody Parker like? People say you two were friends in the old days."

"Cody is good people. He moved back here because he missed the town and his old life."

"I was friends with his father. Frank was always going on about that boy."

"He's getting married soon, so it looks like the Parker name will live on."

Darby shook his head in a sad gesture of the disgust he

was feeling. "I hope the bastard that killed Cody's father and the rest of the family is roasting in hell. Thank God that boy survived."

"Amen to that," Mendez said.

They shook hands goodbye, then Mendez shouted for one of his deputies. The young man that came into the office was white, blond, and looked like he could lift a Buick with one hand.

"Givens, keep an eye on things while I go check out something."

"Okay, and will you be gone long?"

"That depends on what I find," Mendez said, while plucking his hat off the filing cabinet. He was headed into the desert to check out Mr. Darby's story.

AT THE RANCH, SARA RECEIVED A CALL FROM DUKE telling her about the shot that was taken at him in Harlem. She was still seated on the porch with the others. When the call ended, Sara spoke to Cody.

"He's more worried for Lisa than he is for himself, but I think Duke is in over his head."

"Are they still in the penthouse?" Cody asked.

"Yes, and I told him to stay there."

"I'll be flying back to New York with you, and Romeo, I want you to come too."

"Sure, bro, it will be like old times."

"Spenser, I'm sorry to be leaving you here alone, but I'll feel better knowing that you're at the ranch, in case Ordnance Inc. shows up."

"Me guarding the ranch has a sense of déjà vu to it, but how likely do you think an attack now would be?"

"Very unlikely, although I do have concerns about them targeting our wedding day."

Sara scowled. "If that happens, I'll kill them all myself."

"How long will you be in New York City?" Spenser asked.

"I hope it won't take long, and Sara will only be staying for a short time. She has an interview with someone from Blue Truth tomorrow."

Sara caressed Cody's cheek. "I'll also be picking up my wedding dress."

"I can't wait to see you in it," Cody said.

"Just make sure you get back here in time for the wedding."

"I'll be as quick as I can, and Romeo will help."

"Are you flying out today?" Spenser asked. "There's a huge rainstorm headed toward this area tomorrow; it's coming in from the north; you don't want to fly in that kind of weather if you can help it."

"We'll fly out ahead of it," Cody agreed. "And when I get back to New York, I'll deal with Duke's rival, this man, Harkness."

"You said he hired Ordnance Inc., maybe he's hired someone else now, so watch your back," Spenser said.

"I think you're right. Harkness doesn't sound like a man who does his own dirty work. Whoever he hired will wish they had never gotten involved. I'll be flying out of here as Cody Parker, but it's Tanner who will be landing in New York City."

KINFOLK

THE PARKER RANCH, STARK, TEXAS

THE FOLLOWING DAY, THE WIND WAS WHIPPING THE branches of nearby trees as the predicted storm to the north drew closer. Doc looked up from the section of fence he was mending to find a little girl riding toward him on a white horse. The child had long brown hair peeking out from an equestrian riding helmet. When the girl grew closer, she smiled.

"Are you Doc?"

"That's what they call me, little lady, and who might you be?"

"I'm Kelly Alexander... your granddaughter."

Doc's breath caught in his throat as Kelly's words hit home. When he was able to, he spoke in a whisper. "I have a granddaughter?"

"Um-hmm, but I'm the only one, Mom and Dad divorced."

Doc studied the child's face and realized that she resembled his late wife, who was also named Kelly.

"I'm glad you came by, sweetie, and… I'm sorry I haven't been a part of your life."

"Mom said you were very sick the last time she saw you; I always thought that meant you had died."

"I was sick, and for a long time too, but I got better."

"I'm glad," Kelly said, then she dismounted her horse and tied her to the fence. When the child walked over to Doc, she gave him a hug around the waist. "I have a grandpa."

Doc hugged her back, as tears formed in his eyes.

CHIEF STEVEN MENDEZ OF THE STARK POLICE ENTERED the town diner and walked over to the counter while greeting people at the tables. He then stood beside a man whom he had viewed through binoculars the day before.

Mendez had gone to the spot in the desert where meth was being cooked. While lying atop a sand dune, he had observed the four men there for hours. One of those men was at the diner picking up an order to go. When he glanced over and saw the badge pinned to Mendez's slim waist, he stiffened with anxiety.

The waitress and the short order cook said hello to the chief. He smiled and returned their greetings, before ordering a coffee for himself and a piece of pie to go, for his dispatcher. Mendez then turned his gaze on the young man at his side. The guy had tattoos running down each arm and a red scar over his nose.

"Hey there, pardner, are you new in town?"

"Um, yeah, Sheriff."

Mendez smiled. "I'm not a sheriff, son, I'm the chief of police."

"Sorry."

"Don't worry about it; I get that all the time. So, how do you like it here in Stark?"

"It's fine."

"It is, isn't it?" Mendez said, while turning around to face the man fully. "And it's going to stay that way as long as I'm the chief, comprende, pardner?"

The man licked his lips. "I don't know what you mean."

"Yeah, I think you do, and a smart man would pull up stakes and head somewhere else, somewhere far away. Are you and your crew smart men?"

The man nodded. "Yeah, we're smart."

"I hope that's true, for your sake."

The waitress came over to the counter with a large bag of food for the man and a smaller bag for Mendez.

"Let this dude pay first, Gloria; he's in a hurry to get away," Mendez said.

The man paid for his food and left the diner, then he climbed into an old Jeep that was mottled with rust spots.

Chief Mendez left the diner moments later and sipped on his coffee as he watched the meth dealer drive off toward the desert. He nodded to himself. He'd give it a day, then go and take a look to see if they got his message.

A thin smile came over Mendez's face, as he imagined the drug dealer's confusion. If the chief knew they were cooking meth, why didn't he just arrest them instead of issuing a warning? The answer was simple. Incarcerating people cost the town money, scaring them off was cheap. And if they didn't heed the warning? That was when things got interesting.

Mendez entered the station, sat the pie before his dispatcher, and waved off her attempts to pay him for it.

"It's my treat," Mendez said. "I'm feeling generous today."

DOC AND KELLY RODE TO THE RANCH HOUSE, AND KELLY met Spenser. When she told Spenser that his eye patch made him look like a pirate, he laughed.

"I guess it does."

Doc was pouring Kelly a glass of orange juice when her cell phone rang. When she saw that it was her mother calling, she winced. "It's Mom."

"Kelly, where are you?"

"I... I cut across the Kinney Ranch... I wanted to see Grandpa."

"You're at the Parker ranch?"

"Yes."

"I told you to stay away from there."

"But Mom, I really wanted to see Grandpa, and I did, and he's nice."

"Listen to me, young lady, come home right now."

"Why?"

"Because I said so, that's why."

"Yes, ma'am."

Kelly put away her phone and stood. "Mom says I have to come home now."

"Drink your juice first; it's hot out there."

"Why doesn't Mom like you?"

Doc swallowed hard before saying, "I wasn't a good father to her; I was never there when she needed me."

Kelly reached out and took his hand. "You're here now."

Doc smiled. "Yes, and I'm so glad that I got to meet you."

EMERGING FROM THE HOUSE, DOC WAS SURPRISED TO SEE how much windier it had become. The approaching storm was an ominous black mass in the sky to the north.

Kelly climbed onto her horse, then leaned over and planted a kiss on Doc's cheek. "Goodbye, Grandpa."

"Goodbye, honey, and tell your mom I said hi."

Kelly rode off to the east to take a route that would have her going over the land Cody recently acquired. Doc watched her go, while feeling both joy and sadness. After she disappeared from sight within the dust cloud being stirred up by wind, Doc headed into the stable to check on Sara's horse. The speckled mare looked well again, and Doc decided to brush her down.

It was as he was grooming the horse that a memory came to him concerning the land to the east.

"Oh my God," he whispered, as he dropped the brush.

With surprising speed for an old man, Doc saddled up the fastest horse in the stable and was soon rushing off in pursuit of Kelly. If what he feared was about to happen, he prayed he'd not be too late to save her.

NOT THIS TIME

NEW YORK CITY

TANNER AND SARA ARRIVED AT THE PENTHOUSE WITH Romeo at their side. While Sara gave Romeo a tour of the penthouse and settled him into a bedroom, Tanner spoke with Duke inside the home's office.

"There was only one shot?"

"That's right, Tanner, and I felt the bullet as it passed by me."

"Hmm, it makes me wonder if someone was just trying to frighten you."

"If that was their plan it worked. And I've got news; I know who Harkness hired to help him."

"Who?"

"It's a guy they call the Magic Man."

"Are you serious?"

"That's what he calls himself. One of my sources says that he usually does business out on the west coast, around the Seattle area. They also say he's never failed."

"He's an assassin I've never heard of."

"No, he's not an assassin. He's some kind of coordinator. He takes the contracts, then figures out the best way to make the hit."

"And yet, his hitter missed you; he doesn't sound like he'll be much of a problem."

Duke grimaced. "There's more bad news, my guy says that I'm not the Magic Man's target—you are."

Understanding flashed across Tanner's face. "Ah, Healy must have let Harkness know that I'm protecting you, so Harkness decided to hire a heavy hitter, or possibly Healy himself is behind this."

"Who's Healy?"

"Never mind, and don't worry, I'll handle Harkness and this Magic Man."

"I'm sorry you got dragged into this, and I apologize for staying here so long."

"You didn't drag me into this, I volunteered, and as for staying here, we've plenty of room."

"I do have some good news. Lisa has completed three of the masks."

"That's perfect timing. I'll need to use them while I'm here."

"Who are they for?"

"For me; I'll be wearing one."

Duke cocked his head. "I don't get it."

"You don't have to."

"That's true."

As an idea occurred to Tanner, he asked Duke a question. "If I described someone to Lisa, could she make a mask of their face."

"If she sketched it out first, and she's good at that."

"It would also have to be a rush job, and it won't need to be as detailed as the other masks."

"I'm sure she'll be willing to give it a go."

Romeo and Sara returned from their tour of the penthouse. Romeo was smiling.

"Dude, this place rocks."

"We'll be holding onto it, and you and Nadya can use it whenever you come to the city. By the way, this is Duke."

Romeo smiled as he offered his hand. "I've heard about you, Duke. Tanner says that you can get anything."

"He's one of my best customers," Duke said, and afterward, he excused himself.

"Romeo and I will be headed out soon, Sara, and he'll need to take your car tomorrow."

"Why use separate cars?"

"I think whoever shot at Duke did so to see where he would run to. If so, he led them back here."

"But why would they do that when they could have just killed him?"

"Duke is no longer Harkness's main target, I am. Harkness knows he has to get rid of me before he can force Duke to give up his contacts and customer list, otherwise, I would kill him for hurting Duke."

Romeo nodded in understanding. "You want me to follow the follower?"

"That's right, and Harkness has hired someone else to handle the problem."

"A hitter?"

"You're going to like this; the guy calls himself the Magic Man; Duke says that he plans the hits and lets other people carry them out."

"Another fool out to kill you," Sara sighed.

"The Magic Man will be more like a useful idiot; I'll play him and Harkness like pawns to throw Blue Truth off my trail."

"I have an appointment to meet with a Blue Truth representative tomorrow at ten a.m."

"You know what to do?"

"Yes, I only hope the woman buys my story."

"She'll buy it, and even if she doesn't, I'll be giving her another story to believe soon. One that will make sure the law continues to think of me as a myth."

After a visit to see Lisa and get her started on the new mask, Tanner and Sara kissed goodbye, and then he and Romeo left the penthouse by using the private elevator.

In Stark, Kelly was riding her horse inside a narrow gully when she looked behind her and saw something traveling her way in the distance. At first, she wasn't sure what it was, only that it was as wide as the gully and moving fast. When the sound reached her, she understood that it was water, and a moment later it was rushing past the legs of her horse, Princess, while rising higher.

"Princess, we have to get out of here."

The sides of the gully weren't high, only about six feet, but they were too steep for her animal to climb. Kelly urged the horse to move faster along the depression, to where it flattened out again near their home, but Princess was panicky and stamping in place. Meanwhile, the water grew higher, as rains from the north washed down along the gully.

The memory Doc had recalled concerned the gullies on the Kinney ranch. Whenever there was heavy rain to the north, they flooded with water. When dry, they were convenient to ride in, rather than dodging your horse around the brush, which the abandoned ranch had in plentiful amounts.

The spooked horse tossed Kelly from the saddle and the little girl fell into the rising surge of liquid with a scream. Kelly was a good swimmer, but the current was too much for her and she was carried along, while being buffeted against chunks of debris that were in the water.

From up ahead came a loud crash. A tree with weakened roots had succumbed to the high winds and had fallen across the gully. Its branches touched the other side, forming a natural bridge. Kelly was headed for a collision course with its trunk.

She was screaming in dread in anticipation of the impact when she was grabbed by her collar. It was Doc. The old man had thrown himself to the ground on the edge of the gully and stretched out an arm to grab his granddaughter.

"I've got you, honey, I've——" Doc's words were cut short as the flow proved too strong. With his hand still gripping Kelly's collar, he was dragged into the water by the stream's momentum. The unexpected immersion caused him to take in some water and he bobbed back to the surface while sputtering.

"Grandpa, watch your head!"

The warning came too late. Doc smashed into the tree that was straddling the gully and a gash appeared at the rear of his head. Despite the pain and the shock of impact, he had managed to hold on to Kelly. His back and shoulders were continually being slammed against the tree, but it was a blessing in disguise.

"Kelly, crawl on me and get up onto the tree."

The little girl did as suggested, but it took much effort. By the time she was up on the tree, Doc was struggling to stay conscious. The blow to his skull had him seeing double and the continuous battering against the trunk was leaving him bruised and aching.

"Grandpa, climb up too!"

"I don't have the strength, honey," Doc said, and in a voice so weak that Kelly barely heard it. She took out her phone to call her mother and saw that it was dead. Being immersed in the water had ruined the device.

"Crawl," Doc told her. "Crawl to safety."

Kelly was reluctant to leave Doc but knew she needed to get help. After reaching the other side safely, she called out to him. "I'm going to run home and get Mom."

Doc couldn't answer her. He was clinging to the tree while fighting to keep his eyes open. As Kelly ran home to get her mother, Doc slipped beneath the water.

DR. BETH ALEXANDER RODE HER HORSE AS HARD AS SHE dared as her daughter clung to her. Chills passed through Beth. She didn't know if they were caused by Kelly's wet clothing pressed against her back or whether it was a result of the fear she felt for her father's safety.

Kelly had explained what had happened in the gully. Beth felt dread at the thought of her father drowning and was filled with gratitude that he had saved her precious daughter from the same fate.

"Over there, Mom, where that tree fell across."

Beth guided the horse to the tree and dismounted while carrying a length of rope. When she saw the empty water rushing beneath the tree, a soft sound of despair left her.

"Grandpa's gone," Kelly whispered, and she and her mother looked southward along the gully.

"He must have been carried along," Beth said. "Let's get back on the horse and look for him."

They rode along the gully, as overhead, the sky grew darker with the storm growing closer. The atmosphere of the weather matched the increasing dread that Beth was feeling.

When a man's voice called to them from the other side of the gully Beth brought the horse to a stop.

It was Spenser. He was sitting in shadows with his back against a tree, and Doc was with him. Behind them, farther into the trees was a horse tied up to a low branch.

Spenser had seen Doc rushing away on a horse like he was in the Kentucky Derby and wondered what had lit such a fire under the old man. After saddling up another horse, Spenser went in pursuit. By the time he arrived at the gully, Doc had lost consciousness and was being carried along on his back in the rushing water.

Spenser raced ahead to a narrow section of the gully and was able to grab hold of Doc's ankle and pull him out. After turning Doc onto his stomach to get any water out of his lungs, Spenser was about to perform CPR when Doc revived while sputtering out more fluid.

Spenser asked about Kelly and was told she was all right. However, Doc's cognizance lasted only seconds before he passed out again, due to the concussion he'd sustained from his impact with the tree. Spenser had called for an ambulance, then spotted Beth on the other side of the gully.

Beth pointed at her father. "Is he...?"

"He's alive but has a head injury. I would bet he's also exhausted from his time in the water."

"Did you save him, Spenser?" Kelly called out.

"I followed when I saw him take off from the ranch as if he were on fire. Did he come after you to warn you about the flash flood?"

Kelly nodded. "Grandpa saved me, but I think my horse drowned."

"She's fine, Kelly; I passed her on the way here, along

with Doc's horse. Once the ambulance comes, I'll go look for them."

Beth made a sound of frustration while looking at the water. She wanted to go to her father and check his condition, but the twelve-foot gap was keeping them separated.

"If my father wakes, tell him we'll see him at the hospital."

"I'll tell him."

"Your name is Spenser?"

"Yes."

"Thank you for rescuing him, for saving my dad."

"Cody left me here to take care of things; this time I didn't fail."

"This time?"

"It doesn't matter, and I'll tell your father what you said when he wakes."

Beth reached back and gave Kelly's hand a squeeze, then urged the horse to the right as she rushed back to their house. Tears stung her eyes. They were tears of gratitude. She realized that she had come close to losing not only her father, but her daughter as well.

"Kelly, we'll stop home first so you can change into dry clothes, then we'll head to the hospital."

"All right, and Mom?"

"Yes, sweetie?"

"Please don't be mad at Grandpa again."

"That's in the past, honey," Beth said, as she urged the horse to head for home.

THEY MEET AT LAST

NEW YORK CITY

PULLO AND ROMEO WERE BOTH GRINNING AS THEY SHOOK hands inside Joe's office at Johnny R's. They had heard a lot about each other from Tanner over the years, but this is the first time they'd met.

"Tanner says you're as deadly as he is," Pullo said.

"Dude, no one is as deadly as Tanner, and that's been true for a long time."

"Don't let Romeo's surfer guy attitude fool you, Joe. Romeo is no joke when it comes to killing."

"The next time I need some work done in Florida I'll give him a call," Pullo said. Then, he went on to tell Tanner about his meeting with Derek Warner.

"Is Ivanov around, Joe?"

"He's downstairs taking an inventory. Should I call him up here?"

"I'll go to him. If he'll do me a favor, it will help convince Blue Truth that I don't exist. I'll also ask Ivanov about this underground organization of vigilantes he says is operating throughout law enforcement."

"All he said was that it's a rumor going around."

"It's an interesting one if true," Tanner said.

Pullo went over to his desk where he unlocked a drawer and took out an envelope, which he held up. It was an invitation to the wedding.

"I was surprised to get this."

Tanner shrugged. "Laurel figured out my real name when I hid her at the ranch years ago. I'll understand if you can't make it there for the wedding."

Joe laughed. "Are you kidding? Laurel would kill me if I didn't take her there. I will have to be slick about it, so no one knows where we went, not even Sammy or Bosco."

"I'm glad you're coming. I had to miss your wedding."

"Yeah, you had gone off to Mexico to kill Alvarado. I was probably the only one who thought you could do it."

"I had help from Spenser, who you'll finally meet at the wedding."

"The guy you're always saying is better than you? Yeah, him I want to meet."

After sharing a beer and more talk, Tanner and Romeo headed back to the penthouse. The next day, they would deal with the Magic Man.

DOC AWOKE TO FIND HIMSELF LYING IN A TREATMENT ROOM at the hospital. At his right, heavy rain lashed at a darkened window as the storm drenched the area. The hospital was in a town that bordered Stark since Stark only had a clinic.

"He's awake, Mom, he's awake."

Hearing Kelly's voice, Doc turned his head and saw his

daughter and granddaughter standing beside him. He sat up and swung his legs off the side of the examination table.

"Kelly, are you all right? Oh, my head."

"You have a concussion, Dad," Beth told him, she followed the words by reaching out to take Doc's hand. "Thank you for saving Kelly. I would have died if anything had happened to my baby."

"I'm glad I got there in time, but how did I wind up here? This is the hospital in Culver, right?"

"Spenser Hawke saved you and pulled you out of the water."

"He did? The man saved my life. When I felt myself passing out, I figured that was it."

"How do you feel, Grandpa?"

Doc looked down at his hand, which Beth was still holding.

"I haven't felt this good in a long time, honey."

"But your head hurts, doesn't it?"

"Yeah, but my heart is aching less."

The doctor appeared from around a curtain and was pleased to see Doc sitting up. He advised the old man to stay the night in the hospital for observation. Doc was against it, but Beth convinced him to stay.

"You're not a young man, you know? Stay in the hospital and rest. If you're worried about the cost, I'll cover it."

"I'm insured through the ranch, but thanks."

Beth leaned over and kissed Doc. "Thank you again, Dad, and I'm sorry I've been so rough on you."

"Honey, I deserved it, but I promise you I'm no longer drinking."

"I believe you."

They stayed with Doc until he was settled inside a

room, and Beth made plans to pick him up once he was released.

Before leaving, Kelly leaned over the bed and kissed Doc on the cheek. "Goodbye, Grandpa, I love you."

"I love you too," Doc said through tears.

14

DOWN IN THE DUMPS

NEW YORK CITY

Tanner and Duke left the penthouse together and went out the lobby doors. After shaking hands, Duke headed back inside, while Tanner walked around to his private garage to get his car.

If someone had followed Duke back to the apartment building, they had likely watched him and Tanner as they stood in front of the lobby doors. Aware that he was the real target, Tanner assumed that he would be followed. That's where Romeo came in. While Tanner was being trailed, Romeo would follow whoever was doing the trailing. If they had set up a sniper in a shooting post, Romeo would handle that as well.

Pulling his car out of the garage, Tanner headed uptown for approximately thirty blocks while taking several turns along the way. After passing an alley located along a side street, Tanner drove into an underground parking garage.

He had spotted a vehicle that might have been tailing him, a green Hyundai, but was unable to get a good look at the driver. All he had was an impression of curly dark hair and sunglasses. There was also a passenger. That man was blond, but again, Tanner couldn't make out any features.

When a man with curly hair and wearing sunglasses began following him on foot as he left the parking garage, Tanner was certain he had been right.

The blond passenger must have stayed with the vehicle and was trailing behind or parked and waiting. The curly-haired guy was across the street and keeping back just on the edge of Tanner's peripheral vision. When Tanner ducked into a café, the man crossed the street. He stood outside the eatery's glass window, while pretending to read the menu taped to the glass.

After ordering a coffee and a hamburger, Tanner tossed money on the counter and asked the waitress where the men's room was. He was directed down a short hallway. As Tanner made the turn into the corridor, the man outside entered the restaurant and took a booth. He made a phone call.

"What's happening?" Dwight asked.

"I followed the guy to a restaurant, and he went inside the men's room. I'll stick with him, and when I get a chance, he's mine."

"Call me back when something happens."

When Tanner hadn't returned fifteen minutes later, the guy went looking for him in the men's room. Tanner was nowhere in sight. The guy was about to check the ladies' room when he noticed that a door at the end of the corridor was sitting ajar.

"Damn it," the man muttered. "He must have made me and split."

He called Dwight again and told him that he may have lost Tanner.

"I'm going to check out the alley, but he must be long gone by now."

"Keep looking for him. If you can't find him, call me and I'll pick you up."

"Right," the man said, and ended the call.

Curly hair went to the end of the hall and pushed the door open to take a look. As he did so, he slid his gun out of its holster. He stepped out into the alley and looked left, to see cars passing by on the street, which was fifty feet away, when he turned his head to the right, a gun barrel was pressed against his forehead.

"Drop the gun or die."

The gun fell from the man's hand. It was a cheap knockoff of a Glock.

"Shit!" the man said.

"That's right, and you've stepped in it."

"Um, take my wallet, buddy."

"Nice try, but you know I'm not a mugger and I know you're working for some clown calling himself Magic Man."

"He just hired me to follow you."

While keeping the gun pressed against the guy's head, Tanner reached over and raised the punk's baggy black T-shirt, to search for more weapons. Other than a switchblade tucked at his back, there were none.

"Where can I find the Magic Man?"

"I don't know, really, but I guess he lives in the Seattle

area somewhere, that's where he usually sends me on jobs."

"Who was the blond guy in the car with you?"

"His name is Dwight. He works for the Magic Man. He's the one who took a shot at your friend yesterday."

"What's your name?"

"I'm Gary Billings."

"My name is Tanner; did you know that?"

"No, Dwight said I was going after a guy named Jones, but he described those eyes of yours. Wait a minute. Are you *Tanner* Tanner? A hit man like me?"

"I prefer the term, trained assassin."

"The son of a bitch. The Magic Man sent me after someone like you and only paid me five grand?"

"You got a free trip to New York City out of it."

Billings attempted a smile. "Uh yeah, and I'll be glad to get back home... you won't have to worry about me coming at you again."

"I know that," Tanner said. He raised the gun and brought it down swiftly three times against the thug's left temple. Billings grunted before falling to the ground. A glance at the street revealed that no one passing by in a car had taken any notice, and no pedestrians had stopped to gawk.

The alley curved at its end, where a dumpster was placed back there against a brick wall, sitting on an angle. Tanner dragged Gary Billings toward the dumpster and proceeded to smother him by covering his nose and mouth. Because of the injury to his head, the man never woke. Once he was dead, Tanner lifted him up, intending to toss him into the dumpster. That was when he remembered to take the guy's cell phone. There was always a chance of finding information on it.

With the dead man's phone in his pocket, Tanner

tossed the body into the dumpster, followed by the cheap gun. Because of Billing's weight, he sank beneath the numerous green garbage bags from the café.

As he walked down the alley, Tanner took out his phone and called Romeo.

"Hey bro, I'm watching a blond guy in a Hyundai. He dropped off a dude with curly hair to follow you when you left the parking garage, but I'm betting you're aware of that."

"He's been handled. Now I guess I'll have to wait for them to send someone else. You stay on the guy in the Hyundai."

"You got it."

Tanner ended the call then watched as a garbage truck reversed to back down the alleyway. It was time to pick up the trash and ferry it to a landfill. Gary Billings was sent to New York on a contract. He would become a part of New York forever.

15

BE CAREFUL, FOR MY SAKE

SEATTLE, WASHINGTON

THE MAGIC MAN, DR. JONATHON BAXTER, WAS SITTING IN his backyard when Dwight's call came in.

"Tanner took out your first hitter."

"Tell me how he did it?"

Dwight went on to describe how Tanner lured Billings to the rear of the restaurant.

"Are you sure he's dead?"

"He's not answering his phone, so I doubt he's all right."

"Tell me your impressions of Tanner."

"I only saw him at a distance, but I see what people mean about those eyes of his. The guy looks like no one you want to fuck with."

The Magic Man rose from his seat to grab a watering can. "He's met his match in me. I'll place a call. Tanner will be facing multiple opponents next time."

"More than one guy?"

"There are three of them; they're young, work together, and are said to be quite lethal. They should give Tanner more trouble than our friend Billings did."

"When will they contact me?"

"They're already in New York City; I'll have them call you within the hour. I'll also let them know to expect Tanner to come at them circuitously. The man seems to be fond of misdirection."

"And what if these guys fail, what then?"

"I'll be upping the talent. Fontaine is on his way to New York City; he should arrive there tonight."

Dwight laughed. "You've sent him here? I guess you don't expect much from the three guys we'll be using."

"They may succeed but given Tanner's reputation I thought it prudent to send Fontaine."

"Oh, yeah, he's good, and he just handled that lawyer, Rupert."

"Fontaine is excellent, and with you helping out, I expect Tanner to be dead by tomorrow."

"I hope so, the guy worries me."

"Be careful, Dwight. You would be hard to replace."

"I like you too, Jonathon, and you're fun to work for."

"Keep in touch."

After putting his phone in his pocket, Baxter began watering his plants. He was getting paid a hundred-thousand dollars to kill Tanner, and he never had to leave his home. As he recalled Dwight's words, worry lines appeared on his forehead. After setting down the watering can, he called his assistant back.

"What's up?"

"Don't take any more chances by trying to observe Tanner up close. Let Fontaine take the risks."

"All right, but I still want a crack at Tanner if everyone

else fails. Whoever pulls the trigger on him will be famous in the underworld."

"We'll see, just make certain that he doesn't get to you."

The Magic Man wasn't worried about Dwight's safety; he was concerned that Tanner might torture his assistant and make him reveal the Magic Man's location.

TRUST ME, TANNER IS A MYTH

NEW YORK CITY

Sofia Diaz arrived at the hotel coffee shop early for her interview with ex-FBI Agent Sara Blake. When Sara entered, Diaz recognized her immediately from the photo she'd been given. Diaz waved her over to the table she was seated at. She felt a pang of envy while taking in the younger woman's figure.

Diaz was squat and chunky and had been so since she was a girl. Although she had grown to accept her appearance, she nevertheless wished she had a body like Sara's. The face matched the form, and when Sara approached her, Diaz was treated to a dazzling smile.

"Sofia Diaz?"

"Yes, Miss Blake, and thank you for agreeing to meet with me."

"It's my pleasure. I'm a fan of your organization and rarely miss the TV show. I'd also like to keep you from wasting your time."

"Are you speaking of Tanner?"

"Yes."

"What do you know about him?"

Sara's reply was delayed as the waiter came over. She ordered a coffee, while Diaz requested a piece of cherry pie to complement her tea. Even as she asked for the dessert, a part of her mind whispered to Diaz. "This is why you're not slim." It was a voice as familiar as her own, and Diaz had learned to ignore it. Good cherry pie was heaven.

"I spent years looking for Tanner, and even believed that I found him once; however, I was chasing after a phantom."

"Explain that please."

The waiter returned and sat the pie and the coffee on the table. After making certain that the women needed nothing else, the man went to attend to other duties.

"There is a Tanner, and there has been for over a hundred years, but it's a name used by many men. It's the reason why he has the reputation of being unstoppable and a consummate assassin. Whenever one of the men using the name dies, another takes his place. By referring to yourself as Tanner, those hiring you to kill someone will pay more, because they believe they're hiring this supreme assassin."

Diaz read from a computer tablet that was on the table next to her pie.

"'Tanner is real, and I nearly had the bastard dead to rights.'" Diaz looked up at Sara. "Those words were in a report you made in Las Vegas years ago. It was the night the mobster Al Rossetti was killed at his home."

"Yes, and at the time that was what I believed. Weeks later, here in New York, I tracked Tanner down again, or so I thought. I caught a glimpse of the man when he left the scene of the murder of several hoodlums. I saw that it wasn't the same man I'd confronted in Las Vegas, and yet, everyone thought he was Tanner."

"Did you ever see the first man again?"

"My search brought me to a Pennsylvania town called Ridge Creek. At that time, I wounded the man, but he managed to escape me and the FBI by leaping onto a train from an overpass. The wound I gave him was serious. I believe it killed him."

"How can you be sure? Did you ever see him again?"

"Never, but the body of a man was found days later along the tracks in Texas. The corpse had been run over by a freight train, including the skull, so identifying him by his looks was impossible. Still, I believe that was the man I'd shot in Pennsylvania."

"Did you ever search for him again?"

"Yes, in those days I was obsessed with finding Tanner."

"And what did you discover?"

"I found Tanner, another Tanner, or rather, someone using the name. That man was involved in a battle with the mob and killed, or so I was told by a source. That was when I knew I was chasing after a myth, an urban legend."

"What do you make of the tale of Tanner defeating a Mexican cartel leader?"

"It's just that, a tale, and one spread around to enhance Tanner's reputation. The last I heard, some have paid as much as a million dollars to engage his services. The fools who hire a 'Tanner' are being conned."

Diaz shook her head. "I'm not convinced you're correct. There have been many accounts about how unique the man's eyes are."

"Many recent accounts, yes, but if you dig further back in the legend, he's described as having normal eyes. I've even heard accounts where he was portrayed as having long blond hair."

"Blond hair? That I've never come across."

"I have, and more than once."

Diaz reached into her purse and removed a sheet of paper that she unfolded. When Sara looked at it, she had to fight to hide her surprise. Diaz was holding up a scanned copy of one of the flyers that was being passed around years earlier, when Alonzo Alvarado had put a price of two million dollars on Tanner's head. It showed a younger Tanner looking as angry as Sara had ever seen him. The photo was a mugshot snapped by the Mexican authorities when Tanner had been framed for drug possession by Al Rossetti.

Tanner had cautioned Sara to anticipate Diaz to bring it up in conversation, but Sara hadn't expected her to have an actual copy, since few remained in existence.

"The cartel leader Alonzo Alvarado was willing to put up a two-million-dollar reward to eliminate this man. As you can read on the flyer, he referred to him as Tanner."

"I'm aware of that flyer, but there's a story behind it."

"What do you mean?"

"Alvarado was looking for that man, yes, and wanted him dead, but he knew that his name wasn't Tanner. In actuality, that man is someone who Alvarado had thought dead for a long time, and I know him very well."

Diaz leaned forward; her pie forgotten. "You know the man pictured in this flyer?"

Sara brought a photo up on her phone. It was a picture of her and Tanner that had been taken by her sister at their father's house in Connecticut. She passed the phone over to Diaz.

"That man is my fiancé; his name is Cody Parker."

"This is the man in the flyer, and those eyes—he's Tanner!"

Sara took her phone back. "He's not Tanner. He was a victim of Alvarado and survived an attack at sixteen that killed the rest of his family. For a long time, Cody was in the Witness Protection Program, then after hearing that Alvarado was dead, he recently left the program to take his life back."

"But those eyes, he fits the description of Tanner that have been circulating around."

"That's because of that flyer. Alvarado learned through contacts in the government that there was a survivor of the massacre he perpetrated in Texas years ago. Knowing that Cody was in the Witness Protection Program and out of his reach, he came up with a plan to have him hunted down by making it seem that he was the mythical assassin known as Tanner. The plan nearly worked, and Cody was lucky to survive an attack at the location where the marshals had placed him. We still fear that someone may attack him someday."

"That doesn't explain the mugshot that was taken inside a Mexican prison."

"Alvarado faked that, as well as the arrest for drug possession. Miss Diaz, if Cody had been imprisoned for drug possession in Mexico, how could he have escaped?"

"It happens, not often, but it's possible."

"Often through the use of bribes or threats made to guards by drug cartels. Alvarado ran one of those cartels; it was an easy matter for him to fabricate that arrest and fake that flyer. But don't take my word, you can ask the U.S. Marshals that were in charge of relocating Cody. They'll tell you that he was nowhere near Mexico during that time."

"I will have to verify all this."

"I assumed that. Cody spoke to the marshals and asked that they speak to you in confidence." Sara passed across a slip of paper with a number on it. "If you'll call that number, you'll have your questions answered."

Diaz looked down at the paper, then at Sara's phone. "May I have a copy of that photo?"

"I'm sorry, but no, the marshals advised us against that. They weren't happy about my agreeing to meet with you either; however, having been an investigator, I know how frustrating it is to waste time on a dead-end case. I wanted to save Blue Truth from doing that."

"I would love to speak to your fiancé, even by phone."

"I'm sorry, but no. Cody just wants to put the past behind him and move on. The marshals are also against him speaking to anyone. Miss Diaz, Tanner really is nothing more than a story, and that's the truth you've been looking for."

The table grew silent as Sofia mulled over Sara's words. Then, she had a question.

"There have been recent and credible reports of a man matching your fiancé's description at the scene of several murders. How do you account for that?"

Sara held up her hands with the palms facing up. "I have no idea. Cody is a gentle man who only wants to reclaim the life that was stolen from him. Perhaps someone out there resembles him greatly."

Diaz moved her head in a gesture of agreement. "I actually know of a man like that. He's the husband of the criminal profiler Jessica White. I've met him in person, his eyes are very similar to those of Mr. Parker."

"Then perhaps there are other men with similar eyes, or maybe those witnesses were influenced by having seen that flyer you have."

Sofia looked down at the flyer. "Alvarado's plan was evil but ingenious. He must have hated Mr. Parker deeply."

"The man was a monster who nearly ruined Cody's life. By putting out that flyer with such a large reward, he added fuel to the Tanner legend, as a way to make sure Cody was hunted like an animal. When Alvarado was killed and replaced by a rival, the credit went to Tanner."

"How did you meet your fiancé, Miss Blake?"

Sara sighed. "I was following a tip that the man matching the face shown on that flyer was seen in—well, I'll just say that Cody was where the marshals had placed him. I was also certain that I had found Tanner at last, then I realized my mistake. And after getting to know Cody, we fell in love."

Sofia used her fork to break off a piece of her pie. "You've given us a lot to think about, Miss Blake. And yes, I think you have saved us from wasting a lot of time."

Sara smiled. "I'm glad I could help."

17

CRUEL FATE

NEW YORK CITY

IN NEW YORK CITY, SARA RETURNED TO THE PENTHOUSE and found Tanner in the office. She filled him in on her meeting with Sofia Diaz.

"She had one of the flyers, huh? I'm sure a few of those things will be out there for years."

"I hope this plan of yours works. If it doesn't, Blue Truth will now know who you are and where to find you. That would be disastrous in so many ways that it boggles my mind. For starters, we'd be on the run and could never claim the ranch again."

"I know revealing my identity was a risk, but Diaz and her friends at Blue Truth would have to believe that if I was really Tanner, I would never expose myself the way we did. It's reverse psychology, but it often works. The next step in the plan will make them take me off the list of possible Tanners for certain."

"How is part two coming along?"

"It's ready to be used."

Tanner tapped at his phone to text Romeo. When he received a reply, he told Sara to get ready for a shock.

After a knock on the office door, Tanner shouted the words, "Come in." The door opened and Sara released a gasp as she saw Tanner standing in the doorway. It was Romeo wearing one of the Tanner masks that Duke's daughter Lisa had designed. Sara went toward Romeo with her mouth hanging open in awe.

"I expected the mask to look like you, but Lisa got the eyes right as well. How did she do that?"

"They're like little one-way mirrors, Sara," Romeo said. "I can see out, but to you they look like Cody's eyes."

Sara touched Romeo on the cheek to feel the mask. "It's incredible."

"It should fool Blue Truth and the rest of law enforcement, that is, once we put on a show."

"To do that, you'll need to find the men who are threatening Duke, Harkness and—what's the man calling himself again?"

"The Magic Man, the dude must think he's something special," Romeo said.

Hearing his surfer dude voice coming out of Tanner's mouth was bizarre to Sara.

"Yes, those two."

"Zoe Farnsworth tracked a man named Jared Harkness to Chicago from here in New York. He's been arrested several times for various criminal activities and once worked for Hexalcorp. He's staying at a hotel there, likely waiting until he gets a message that Duke and I are dead."

"He's in Chicago?" Sara said. "Is there a connection between Harkness and Ordnance Inc.?"

"I wondered about that too, and I'll be talking to Michael

and Kate Barlow soon. Maybe they'll have information for me. Ordnance Inc. was once part of Hexalcorp; there's a good chance that Harkness and Trevor Healy know each other."

"If so, and Healy is behind this Magic Man, then that would mean he's broken the truce you have."

"Proving that would be difficult, and since he's using a surrogate, Healy can deny involvement. Still, it's just one more sign that an attack is on the horizon."

"And what happened today?" Sara asked.

"They sent an assassin after me and I handled him easily, a bit too easily. I think the Magic Man is testing me, to learn how I think. Duke said he's the type who figures out the best method of attack."

"He'll send someone else, and now they know where to find you."

"Yes, but I'll be using that to my advantage, with Romeo's help."

"Whatever you need, bro." Romeo scratched at his neck. "I'm going to go take this thing off, it makes me sweat, but I want to borrow it when Halloween comes around."

After Romeo left the office, Sara sat on the edge of the desk and smiled at Tanner.

"We're getting married in five days."

"Excited?"

"I am, and I have my dress. You make sure you return to the ranch on time... and in one piece."

"I'll settle things with Harkness and his people in the next couple of days and be back at the ranch."

"I'm glad you have Romeo helping you, and it's sad what happened between Amy and Spenser."

"I really thought she was right for him, but you never know."

Sara leaned over and kissed him. "We're right for each other."

"Amazingly so, you were the last woman I would have ever thought I'd marry. But you're actually very sweet when you're not out to kill me."

Sara laughed. "My sister still finds it odd that we're a couple."

Tanner stood and took Sara in his arms. "We're going to have a good life together in Stark. I swear that to you."

"Fate was very unkind to you during your early years. I think you're owed a happy ending."

Tanner hugged Sara a little tighter, while praying that she was right.

18

ROUND TWO

Later that day, Romeo left the penthouse before Tanner and spotted Dwight parked down the street. The Magic Man's flunky was using binoculars to keep watch for Tanner. When Dwight pressed buttons on his phone and a teen parked in front of a hydrant answered his cell a moment later, Romeo watched the two of them. He became convinced they were talking to each other.

The man at the hydrant wasn't alone. There were two other guys in the car, and they looked to be in their late teens as well. Romeo was struck by how young they were, then remembered that he and Cody had been even younger when they began their apprenticeship with Spenser.

Romeo made a call to Tanner. "It looks like there are three more hitters after you."

"A team?"

"Yeah, all young punks, I'll sneak a few photos and send them to you."

"Good. Once I know what they look like, I'll be taking a little ride."

"I'm sure they'll follow you. Do you want any help?"

"I need you to stick with the blond guy. He must be coordinating things for the Magic Man. Once I get rid of the three you spotted, the blond man might meet with a new hitter. I've a feeling the next assassin won't be a pushover."

"You think this Magic Man will throw more guys at you?"

"Yeah, until he feels he knows me well enough to come up with a plan."

Romeo laughed. "If this keeps up, he'll eventually have to hire you to kill yourself."

TANNER LEFT THE PENTHOUSE A SHORT TIME LATER BY exiting the front of the building and walking around to his private garage. Duke had arranged for him to have a car from a used car lot that was similar in appearance to his own car. Duke had a relationship with the owner of the used car lot and did business with the man often. When the time was right, the car lot would report the vehicle as having been stolen. If Tanner was able to return it without an incident occurring, so much the better.

This time, Tanner had no trouble tracking the men following him, since they only kept one car between themselves and Tanner. He also had a good look at Dwight via his rearview mirror while stopped at a traffic light.

Since Romeo was following Dwight, Tanner knew that he was close by, but he didn't spot him more than once as Romeo tracked Dwight.

As he had done earlier, Tanner drove into an underground parking garage. He wore a black cap with a long bill and mirrored sunglasses. The attendant inside the booth was wearing a red jacket with the logo of the parking garage on its back. The logo displayed a group of cars neatly lined-up inside a circle.

As Tanner parked on the lowest level, Romeo called. "Heads up, bro. Those three that were following you just knocked out the guy that was in the booth of the garage."

"How did it happen?"

"One of those dudes is huge. He knocked the attendant out cold with one punch."

"It sounds like somebody likes to use their fists; I'll give him a chance to do it again."

"Be careful, Cody."

"I'll call you soon."

There was a second attendant in the garage. Tanner left his car and approached the man as he was walking the lower level to check on the vehicles. When the man saw the gun in Tanner's hand, he asked him if he wanted his phone and wallet.

"You can keep them, but I will take that jacket you're wearing."

"Huh?"

"Let me have it, and be quick about it; I'll also need you to hide."

THE THREE PUNKS HUNTING TANNER WERE NAMED DAVID, Jesse, and Mick. Mick was the brute that liked to use his fists. They split up to search the garage. When Mick wandered across what he believed was another attendant, he came up behind him and reared back a fist.

Mick had intended to smash the guy on the side of the head. Instead, the man ducked the punch and pivoted to deliver punishment to Mick's midsection. Mick had thought the man was jabbing him with a fist. It wasn't until he felt the blood that he realized the man had been using a knife. He raised up his hands to plead for mercy then watched with surprise as his assailant turned and sprinted away.

Mick leaned against a car with one hand while the other was pressed against his wounded stomach. The pain was intense, but after a wave of agony passed, he cried out to his friends.

"Dave, Jesse, I need help! The bastard stabbed me."

Mick's two friends ran to him and were shocked when they saw how bloody he was. Jesse, who had acne scars, rotated around like a top as he looked for Tanner.

"Where is he, Mick, where's Tanner?"

The answer to that question came in the form of a gunshot. The bullet that was fired entered Jesse's right cheek and exited out of the back of his skull. As Jesse's body fell, a second shot struck David in the chest, rupturing his heart.

Mick fumbled his gun out and nearly dropped it because of how slippery the blood had made his hands. He fired off several random shots that did nothing more than shatter a car's windshield. He had no idea where Tanner's rounds had been fired from and was hoping to get lucky. He fled from the scene and made it back outside. The keys to the car he had arrived in were in David's pocket. Mick wasn't going to waste time trying to get to them. When he spotted Dwight double-parked down the block, he lumbered toward him while dripping blood from his stab wounds.

"Holy crap! What happened?" Dwight said, as he looked around to see if Mick had been followed by Tanner. He saw no one on foot other than two women leaving a coffee shop.

"Tanner dressed like one of the garage attendants and stabbed me. Get me to a doctor."

"All right, hold on."

"Dave and Jesse are dead, and my gut feels like it's on fire."

Dwight ran a red light as he drove toward a clinic he remembered passing earlier. When he turned his head to speak to Mick, he saw a pair of glassy eyes staring back at him.

"Mick?"

No response, as was typical of a corpse. Dwight drove past the clinic, turned left down a street with factories lining it, and drove around to a rear parking lot. When he was certain there was no one looking at him and no cameras pointed his way, Dwight reached across Mick, open the passenger door, then shoved the body out. As he drove away, he called the Magic Man to report what had happened.

∾

ROMEO FOLLOWED DWIGHT WHILE SPEAKING TO TANNER. "He dumped the dude in the parking lot of a factory. I guess he died."

"As long as he lived long enough to report what happened. By now, the Magic Man should be getting a picture of how I work, or, how I want him to think I work. Then, when I need to, I'll switch tactics."

"Do you think he'll send more hitters?"

"Yeah, but I've had enough of these idiots today. I'll take the subway back to the penthouse and we'll do it again tomorrow."

"I'll follow the blond dude and see where he goes."

"Thanks, Romeo."

"See you later, bro."

As Tanner was putting away his phone, he noticed how dirty the front of his jeans were and brushed them off with his hands. He had crawled beneath a car to stay out of sight while he had fired the shots that killed David and Jesse.

As he neared the subway station, he changed his mind and decided to walk the twenty blocks back to the penthouse. It was a nice day. At least, it was for some.

19

TOO MUCH

NEW YORK CITY

Early the following morning, Tanner went down to the lobby to have a talk with the man who was the building's night doorman. He was a young guy named Stewart who was working his way through law school. Tanner had noticed a habit that Stewart had, and it had given him an idea. Stewart, like everyone else in the building knew Tanner by the name of Thomas Myers.

"A spare uniform jacket, Mr. Myers, yeah, I keep one handy, why do you ask?"

"I want to borrow it. I believe someone has been hired to follow me and I want to throw them off the trail."

"A hundred bucks, but that includes the hat."

Tanner smiled. "You've done this before."

Stewart lowered his voice, although there was no one else around at such an early hour.

"Mr. Farley in 8B likes to fool around with married

123

women. Walking out of here in a doorman's uniform has saved him from a beating more than once. I think I've made about a thousand bucks off him so far."

Tanner passed Stewart a hundred-dollar bill. Stewart held up a finger in a, "wait a minute," gesture, then disappeared into a small room off the lobby. When he returned, he handed Tanner a doorman's jacket and a cap.

"The jacket might be a little tight, but it should fit okay."

"I'll bring it back tonight when you come on shift."

Stewart pocketed the hundred. "That works for me."

THE ASSASSIN NAMED FONTAINE WAS OUTSIDE THE apartment building, around the corner, where he could watch the entrance to the penthouse's private garage.

Dwight had informed him that Tanner had walked around to the roll-up door to take a car out of it the day before. Fontaine thought it likely that Tanner might need a car again, but he had placed Dwight out in front of the building to keep watch in case Tanner left that way instead.

A former Marine sniper, Fontaine liked to kill from a distance. He was set up on the rooftop of a liquor store that offered a good view of the garage's corrugated metal door. If Tanner drove out of there, Fontaine would place a round in his head.

His phone rang. It was Dwight calling.

"You have something to report?"

"No sign of Tanner yet, but the night doorman just got off duty and is headed your way."

"I don't see any pedestrians down there other than several women and an old man with a cane."

"Oh, maybe he went down into the subway. Hey, this is boring; do you do this all the time?"

"It can sometimes take hours before a target shows, even days."

"You've got more patience than I do."

"Enough talk; just keep an eye out for Tanner and— hold on, the garage door is going up. I'll call you back when he's dead."

"I'll listen for the shot," Dwight said.

ON THE ROOF, FONTAINE WAS PEERING THROUGH A VORTEX rifle scope as he waited for a vehicle to emerge from the private garage. He was across the street, lying on his stomach with the rifle supported on a shooting rest. To keep himself hidden from view of the apartments across the avenue he had strung up a blue tarp. The plastic was slung between a giant HVAC unit and an old clothesline pole that someone had rigged up many years earlier.

When more than a minute had passed since the garage door rose, Fontaine wondered what was keeping Tanner from leaving the building. He calmed himself, kept his eye to the scope, and waited patiently.

There could be any number of reasons why Tanner was so slow in leaving. He might be down there talking on the phone, or to someone in person, or he might even be doing something dull, like adding oil to the car. However, he had opened the garage door for a reason; it was likely that he would be pulling out of the garage at some point.

When the tip of a gun was pressed to the back of his head, Fontaine knew he'd been played. After swallowing hard, he spoke in a calm voice. "Hello, Tanner. My name is Fontaine."

"Release the rifle, then sit up on your knees."

"Whatever you say. I'm not looking to die here, and we're both professionals."

"You're a step up from the last few guys the Magic Man sent, I'll give you that."

Fontaine turned his head slowly to look at Tanner and the hole at the end of the gun was pointed at a spot between his eyes. When he saw that Tanner was dressed in a doorman's jacket and cap, he understood how the assassin had gotten by Dwight.

"Like I said, I'm a pro, so I can guess what you want. It's the Magic Man, right?"

"Good guess."

"If you let me walk off this roof, I'll tell you where you can find him."

"You might lie and make up an address."

"And you might go back on your word and kill me."

"Or, I could take you somewhere and torture you until I'm sure you're telling the truth."

"Hmm, I wouldn't want that, so I guess I'll have to trust you. Do we have a deal? I give you the Magic Man and you let me off this roof?"

Tanner nodded once. "I won't kill you; you have my word."

Fontaine turned his whole body around and stood slowly. "The Magic Man is a retired psychiatrist named Jonathon Baxter."

"Why do you know that?"

"I made it my business to know. Baxter never gets involved in the actual work but uses a guy named Dwight Wheatley to help set things up. I followed Dwight back to the Magic Man's house a few months ago after we'd worked on a hit together. You can have him too. Dwight is parked in front of the building, but I don't know where he's staying while in the city."

"I know where to find him, but I didn't know his name."

"I see, tell me, who opened the garage door?"

Tanner held up the remote that he had used on the door.

Fontaine nodded. "I should have thought of that."

"Where can I find the Magic Man?"

Fontaine gave Tanner an address in Seattle, along with a phone number.

"Speaking of phones, let me have yours," Tanner said.

Fontaine passed it over, slowly. "You're really letting me off this roof?" Fontaine glanced over at the edge. "I mean, let me get off the roof alive?"

"That was the deal, but I'm keeping the rifle. It looks like it's been well-cared for."

"It does, doesn't it? I bought it here in New York after I landed, a guy named Harkness arranged it."

"Jared Harkness?"

"That's him."

"I'll be looking him up too; he's the reason you're here."

Fontaine stared at the rifle. "One more thing, Tanner, I'd like to take the rounds out of that gun. Not that I don't trust you, but you might be tempted to use it to put me down once I'm off the roof."

"No, I wouldn't. I said I won't kill you and I won't. Since it doesn't matter, I'll give you the cartridges. While I'm doing that, I want you to lie down again, after I frisk you."

"There's a gun in a holster under my left arm."

"Really? You have a good tailor."

Fontaine smiled. "I like to look my best, you know, for the ladies."

"Move the jacket aside and hand over the gun, holster and all."

Fontaine complied. When Tanner had him unarmed and the cartridges removed from the rifle, he handed the ammunition to Fontaine.

"You'll never see me again, Tanner."

"If I do, you die."

Fontaine gave a slight bow. "You're as good as they say."

"Goodbye, Fontaine."

Fontaine left the roof by walking backwards toward the door and keeping Tanner in view. After he was in the stairwell, he ran down the steps, left the building, and hailed a taxi.

As the vehicle sped away, Fontaine laughed with relief. He was thankful he'd had information about the Magic Man to use to bargain for his life. Even so, he thought that Tanner would kill him. If their places had been reversed, Fontaine would have shot Tanner dead.

I still might someday, Fontaine thought. It had hurt his pride to be taken from behind like that.

The cab let him out in front of the hotel he was staying at in lower Manhattan. As he was headed toward the entrance a guy bumped into him, a blond guy carrying a large package. One of the corners of the parcel must have hit Fontaine on the leg because he felt a sharp pain along his inner thigh.

"Sorry, dude, my fault," the man said, and kept walking.

Fontaine was about to tell the guy to watch where he was going when he felt the wetness running down his leg. It was blood.

The blond man, Romeo, had cut Fontaine's leg, severing the femoral artery.

"No!" Fontaine said. He was a professional killer and understood the wound he'd received gave him only minutes left to live. The taxi that had dropped him off was still at the curb. Fontaine opened the door and slid inside. "Take me to the nearest hospital!"

The cabbie turned around to look at him but couldn't see his bloody leg. "What?"

"I need a hospital!"

"Okay, relax, there's one three blocks from here."

"Hurry!"

The cab made it two blocks before it stopped at a red light with traffic blocking it in. During the short trip, Fontaine had used his tie to form a tourniquet around his thigh. It did little good and blood was pooling on the floor of the cab.

"Damn it. Don't sit at the light I'm dying back here."

"This thing don't fly, buddy. I can't move until everyone else does."

"Where's the hospital?"

The cabby pointed through the windshield at a building across the street and several doors down. A sign proclaimed that there was an entrance to the emergency room. An ambulance was parked in front.

"The hospital is right there, and... what's that odor? It smells like copper."

Fontaine opened the door and lurched out onto the street. Two women walking by backed up in a panic when they saw how bloody he was. With the light still red, Fontaine rushed amid the morning traffic to make it across the street, leaving behind a trail of blood. When he staggered into the ER, he was so relieved he giggled.

As a nurse and an orderly rushed up to him, Fontaine's

legs gave out and he fell down. A moment later, he felt himself slipping away.

"Too much," he whispered.

He was right, he had lost too much blood. Despite the hospital's best efforts, Fontaine died.

20

THE BIG DAY APPROACHES

NEW YORK CITY

AFTER LEAVING THE ROOFTOP WHERE HE'D CONFRONTED Fontaine, Tanner went back to the penthouse's private garage where Sara was waiting in the car. She had her bags, including the box that contained her wedding dress. She was heading back to the Parker ranch, where the nuptials would take place in four days.

Tanner had Fontaine's sniper rifle broken down and wrapped inside the borrowed doorman's jacket. He left the rifle inside the garage and tossed the jacket on the rear seat. He had plans to drop it off at a one-hour dry-cleaning establishment.

"That didn't take long, and I never heard a shot."

"I never fired one. Romeo will handle the hitter."

"I'm glad you brought him and Spenser into your plan."

"It wouldn't work without them," Tanner said, as he pulled out onto the street.

131

"When will you be ending things?"

"Tomorrow, or maybe the next day. It depends on whether this Magic Man clown wants to send another hitter at me."

Sara looked at him sideways. "That's cutting it close to the wedding."

"I know, and I'm sorry, but the good news is that so far the plan is working."

"It has to work. If it doesn't... I don't even want to think about it."

"We might run into Romeo at the airport; he's flying out to Chicago to deal with Harkness."

"I wish I could help in some way."

"Sara, you'll have your hands full getting the ranch ready for the wedding. That reminds me, when are your father and sister flying in?"

"They'll arrive at the ranch the day before the wedding; Daddy is flying them all in."

Tanner smiled. "Between your father, the defense attorney, Jake, the FBI agent, and Joe, the mob boss, it will be an eclectic guest list."

"Not to mention Romeo and Spenser."

"What about White and Jessica?"

"They're definitely coming, so Caleb won't be the only family you'll have there."

Tanner moved amid the morning traffic deftly, although he expected it to slow once they were on the highway during the rush hour.

Sara reached over and gripped his hand. "Promise me you'll be careful. Your part of the plan seems risky."

"It is, but I need to take the chance; I'll also be taking precautions."

"What Spenser calls due diligence?"

"Yes, I see you're picking up our lingo."

"This is going to work, isn't it, Cody?"

"That's right, and in a few days, we'll be on our honeymoon."

Sara gave his hand a squeeze. "And I'll be Mrs. Cody Parker."

～

ONCE AGAIN, DWIGHT FOUND HIMSELF UNABLE TO MAKE contact with an assassin who had been trying to kill Tanner. When he called Baxter in Seattle to report in, the Magic Man asked Dwight to tell him exactly what had occurred.

"I was watching the front of the building. Fontaine was on a roof with a rifle keeping an eye on the garage door. The last thing he said to me was that the door was going up and that he would call me back. I waited to hear a rifle shot… but it never came."

"That's because Tanner outsmarted Fontaine. Start from the beginning, and this time tell me every detail you remember."

Dwight did so, and when he was done, he could hear the glee in the Magic Man's voice.

"The doorman who left the building was Tanner in disguise."

"Seriously?"

"I'd bet on it, and then he fooled Fontaine by opening the garage door. I'm sad to lose such a competent man as Fontaine, but now I know how to kill Tanner."

"What are you going to do, send a team of assassins here to hunt him down?"

"I doubt that would work, no, I'll require only one man, and he won't even need to be armed."

"No gun? How's that going to work?"

"We'll lure him to a location that's been prepared in advance. That's where you come in. Find an abandoned building somewhere that is off the beaten track."

"There's a house up in Harlem that had a recent fire. No one's living there."

"That might suit my needs. Take pictures of it and send them to me."

"You'll have them in an hour."

"And Dwight?"

"Yeah?"

"Buy a good saw, something that runs on a battery. You'll also need a large supply of long nails, or spikes, if you can find them."

"A saw? Spikes? Jonathon, what have you thought of now?"

Baxter's grin was discernable even over the phone. "I've thought of a way to kill Tanner, and the beautiful part is that he'll do it to himself."

MORE MYTH THAN MAN

SAWYER'S CREEK, ARKANSAS

Ex-Philadelphia Homicide Detective Victor Middleton made a right off a two-lane road and turned down a driveway bordered by wildflowers.

Victor had called ahead and spoken to the wife of one of the men he wanted to interview. The woman, Mrs. Hanna Carter, called him back hours later and told him that her husband and brother-in-law would be happy to talk to him.

"They understand that I'll be asking them questions about a man they once knew who called himself Tanner?"

"Oh yeah, they said they'd tell you all about him."

Victor flew out of New York early in the morning and landed in Little Rock just after noon. The drive to Sawyer's Creek was pleasant and the scenery filled with views of farmland and rolling hills. The Carter farm looked well-cared for, and the corn and wheat crops were standing high and healthy above the fertile soil they'd sprouted from.

Hanna and Savannah came out onto the wide front porch to greet him and Victor found the sisters to be charming. By the look of them, they were each about seven months pregnant. Then, he met their husbands, Merle and Earl.

The boys had been cleaning out the stable, and as they walked around the corner of the house, the aroma of the stable followed them.

"Look at you two," Hanna said. "You are not coming in my house with those nasty boots on. Go out back and take them off before you do anything else."

"Yes, ma'am," both men said, then Merle spoke to Middleton. "You came all the way from New York City, right?"

"I did, and I have questions for you concerning a contract killer known as Tanner."

Merle nodded. "We'll tell you all about him, but first I gotta take off these boots. Hanna don't like it when we track horse shit through the house."

"Um, yes, I can imagine she wouldn't."

"Come on inside, Mr. Middleton," Hanna said. "Savannah and I will get you a cup of coffee."

"Thank you, ladies."

Middleton found the old house to be as simple and charming as the women who lived within it. It reminded him of his grandmother's home in South Carolina, which he had visited in the summers as a boy. He was sipping on a good cup of coffee by the time Merle and Earl joined him at the kitchen table. The brothers were in their stocking feet and no longer smelled of horse manure. Since they were both sweaty, that did not mean they weren't giving off an odor.

Merle grabbed two beers from the refrigerator and

handed one to Earl, when he asked Middleton if he wanted a can, the ex-cop declined.

With the brothers settled across from him at the kitchen table, Victor was ready to begin the interview. The men's wives had gone off to see to some of the endless chores that needed doing around the farm. Victor smiled at Merle and Earl. He was aware of their criminal records, and the fact that they had been arrested for petty crimes. It was expected. Anyone who had come in contact with an assassin like Tanner wouldn't likely be a sterling citizen.

Victor had received the report Sofia Diaz filed about her conversation with Sara Blake. Sofia's subsequent conversation with a U.S. Marshal confirmed Miss Blake's story. It seemed a certainty that the man pictured in the flyer that had been circulating years earlier wasn't Tanner. However, Victor still believed that there must be someone operating as an assassin under that name. If such was the case, he was determined to track that man down and bring him to justice.

"Why don't we do this, gentlemen, you tell me what you know about Tanner and I'll ask any questions I might have as we go along, okay?"

"Do we get paid for this?" Earl asked.

"No, Blue Truth doesn't pay for interviews."

"Dang."

"What about that TV show you people got?" Merle said. "Is there a chance we could be on that?"

"That's a possibility, depending on what I learn from you."

"That would be cool. Earl and me ain't never been on TV."

"How did you first meet Tanner?"

"We grabbed him up after he killed Aldo and his crew at this house in Las Vegas a few years back. Aldo was workin' for this fat guy named Rossetti and he and his crew had trapped Tanner inside a house."

"How many men in this crew?"

"Aldo and three guys."

"And this Tanner killed all four of them by himself?"

"He tricked them by hidin' inside an oven."

"An oven? Was it some sort of large oven such as a restaurant might use?"

"Nope, it was just a normal house with a regular oven."

"Is Tanner a short man?"

"He about your height."

"Then, I don't see how he could fit in an oven."

Merle shrugged. "After we caught him and was takin' him to Rossetti to cash in, we asked Tanner how he hid from Aldo."

"And he said that he hid inside an oven?"

"Uh-huh."

"What happened next?"

"Tanner got away from us, which made Rossetti mad, then Tanner showed up later at Rossetti's house in an RV with a dummy drivin'."

"A dummy?"

"You know, like a mannequin, it was sittin' behind the wheel and had on a hood and sunglasses."

"How could the dummy have driven the vehicle? And why would Tanner need an RV?"

Merle shrugged again.

Victor fiddled with a computer tablet, then held it up for the brothers to get a look at. It displayed the mug shot of Tanner that Sofia Diaz had showed Sara.

"Is this the man you know as Tanner?"

The brothers both shook their heads. "That ain't him," Merle said. "The dude we grabbed was older than that and had lighter hair. But I've seen that picture before and know'd he's worth a lot of money to somebody."

"He was, but the man offering the reward died."

"Yeah, that cartel leader, right, but I heard the reward could still be collected."

"You're saying that the two-million-dollar reward is still viable?"

"Viable?"

"Possible to cash in on."

"Oh yeah, but you'd have to go down to Mexico to get it. Who is that guy in the picture? He's got strange eyes."

"It doesn't matter," Victor said, as he put away the tablet. "I know that Tanner is said to have killed Al Rossetti and that you two were present that day. Did you ever see Tanner again?"

"When we was in New York City there was talk that Tanner was there too, but when we saw him, it was a different guy."

"He was another man calling himself Tanner?"

"Yeah, but he and Lars Gruber killed each other in an alley behind the old Cabaret Strip Club, then a few weeks later, another dude was callin' himself Tanner."

"What did that man look like?"

"Nothin' special, and he was a little smaller than the other two, I heard he died after jumpin' on a train in Pennsylvania."

Victor frowned. The legendary Tanner was looking like a myth after all.

"Have you ever come across any other Tanners?"

"We sure have," Earl said. "There's a guy named Tanner Mumfrey who works down at the feed store. He's a little fella too; I'd bet he could fit inside an oven. You want to talk to him?"

Victor grabbed his computer tablet and stood. "I don't

think I need anymore. Thank you for your time, gentlemen, and tell your wives goodbye for me."

MERLE AND EARL STOOD ON THE PORCH AS THEY WATCHED Victor Middleton drive away. After sharing a laugh, Merle went into the house and used the landline phone to call the number he'd been given.

"Hello?"

"It's Merle, Joe. One of them guys from Blue Truth just left here."

"How did it go?" Pullo asked.

"We told him that Tanner was a bunch of different fellas. He didn't like hearin' that."

"You boys did good, thanks."

"How's my little nephew Johnny doing?"

"The kid is great, Merle."

"How come you didn't name him after me?"

"One Merle is enough."

"Tell Laurel we said hey to her."

"I'll do that, and I'll let Tanner know he owes you one."

"Tanner can pay us by stayin' away. He's bad luck for us."

"He'll be happy to leave you alone. Goodbye, Merle."

As Merle hung up the phone, Earl asked him a question.

"Is Tanner payin' us for doin' this?"

"No."

"Dang."

VICTOR WAS HEADED FOR THE AIRPORT WHEN THE CALL came in from Derek Warner. Someone had tipped them to the fact that a hit man calling himself Tanner had a contract to kill someone named Harkness.

"How reliable is this tip?" Victor asked.

"I got it from an ex-FBI agent named Tamir Ivanov. He works at Pullo's strip club as a bartender and overheard some talk. He knows we're hunting Tanner and gave me the tip."

"It's not much to go on, but maybe it will lead to something."

"The researchers are looking into it, but there are over fifteen thousand people named Harkness. How did your interview go?"

"The two brothers say that they've known three different men who have used the name Tanner, four if you count the guy who works at the feed store."

"What?"

Victor laughed. "It doesn't matter, and I'll see you tomorrow morning in New York."

"Have a good flight home, Victor."

"Thanks, Derek." Victor put away his phone. As he drove toward the airport, he was considering what they would look into next. Although no official conclusions had been reached, in his mind, the Tanner myth was a dead-end.

22

LAW & ORDER

STARK, TEXAS

Stark Chief of Police Steven Mendez laid on a hill with a pair of binoculars as he watched the group of meth dealers he had run out of his town. There were four of them, and they were busy brewing their toxic product.

The gang had dismantled their shack and moved it a mile into the outskirts of the town of Culver. It was within sight of another shack, an ancient structure that was old when Mendez's father was born. As boys, he and Cody Parker had used it as a clubhouse of sorts. Mendez had warned one of the drug dealers to get out of his town, and this is where they had settled.

I guess they didn't receive my message, Mendez thought. While it was true that the meth dealers were no longer in his town, technically, by staying so close their poison would certainly be peddled on the streets of Stark. That is, if Mendez didn't do something about it.

The chief left the hill and went back to his vehicle. Once there, he accessed a hidden compartment at the rear, beneath a tire well. From that compartment he removed three guns. Mendez stuck one pistol behind his back, under his waistband, another was secured in front, and the third weapon he gripped in his hand, with the selector switch set to fire a burst of three shots.

He moved on foot while circling the shack. There was a man outside it, supposedly keeping watch, although he spent more time playing a game on his phone then he did looking around for signs of anyone approaching. The guy had long, unruly sandy hair, a goatee, and wore jeans so old that they were almost faded white from wear and washing.

Mendez drew nearer to the man and secured an observation post behind a wide cactus. It was a hot day and a wasp kept buzzing around his head, but Mendez hardly noticed. His attention was riveted on the man guarding the shack. A little sunburn and a sting wouldn't kill you. The same could not be said about the weapon strapped onto the belt of the man he was watching.

Mendez had to be patient for several minutes until an opportunity to strike came. But that was okay, for Mendez had been prepared to wait much longer. He had developed the ability to be patient while working undercover in the DEA.

The man outside the shack placed his phone in his pocket and walked toward the cactus Mendez was hidden behind, when he got within a few feet of it, he began zipping down his pants to take a leak.

"You piss on me and I'll make you wish you hadn't," Mendez told him.

The drug dealer jumped backwards as Mendez stood from his crouch and came at him while pointing a gun.

"Easy, pardner, no one has to get hurt here. Don't go for that gun on your hip."

"Hey, officer, dude don't shoot me. I'm... I'm not with those guys in the shack... I was just out walking in the desert."

"Sure you were. Now, put those hands up and turn around."

The man did as he was told. Mendez struck him with a billy club and watched him go down. He then struck him again. After dragging the meth merchant behind the cactus, Mendez moved over to the shack, while being careful to stay downwind from the smoke coming out of its roof.

More patience was required, as he was still outnumbered three to one. However, the next man emerged from the shack only a few minutes later. Mendez hit him on the side of the head with the billy club and watched him fall. He was a large guy with a red face and a pug nose. The blow to the head had only stunned him. He looked up at Mendez and was about to cry out when the chief gave him a hard kick to the face. The pug nose broke as the blow rendered the man unconscious. Unfortunately, the guy fell back against the door of the shack and rattled it.

"What are you doing out there, Frank?" called a voice from inside the shack. When there was no answer, Mendez knew the owner of the voice would come out to look around. Mendez put away the club and readied his gun in both hands, while moving to the side of the shack.

Two men emerged a few moments later, both had weapons holstered, one of them was the tattooed man from the diner. Mendez killed him first. The chief fired three rounds into the guy's side as he was turning to look his way. The second man was the meth cook. He was wearing an apron and gloves and was squinting at the bright sunlight.

He was raising his hands up in surrender when Mendez used a second gun to shoot him twice in the chest and once in the head. Moving on, Mendez used the third weapon that he had tucked behind his back to shoot the men he had rendered unconscious. The man with the pug nose grunted as a bullet entered his throat but didn't open his eyes. Those eyes would never open again.

With the men dead, Mendez removed their guns and fired them off once or twice before tossing them on the ground near their owners. Having done what he came out into the desert to do, Mendez entered the lab. There was a supply of meth already made and more cooking.

A short search uncovered over twelve thousand in cash and a pound of marijuana. Mendez would burn the weed a little at a time during his leisure hours, as for the cash, it would find its way into the donation boxes of several churches in town.

Before leaving the shack, Mendez rigged the equipment inside so that it would overheat and cause an explosion. That would bring the Culver police to the scene. Being the chief of a neighboring town, Mendez would drive around the hill that his vehicle was parked behind as if he had just arrived. He would be at the scene when the Culver P.D. showed up.

As for the drug dealers, he had given them a chance to move on. They had wasted it, and Mendez had wasted them. Stark was his town and he'd be damned if he was going to let it go to hell on his watch, no sir.

Mendez put the guns back in their hidden compartment, stripped off the gloves he wore, then sat in his unit and waited for the explosion to occur. He had no idea that his actions had been observed and recorded.

WHEN HE WAS CERTAIN THE CHIEF WAS GONE AND OUT OF sight of the ramshackle structure he was in, Spenser led Kelly's horse away from the area. He had been unable to locate the animal before the storm hit and had no luck the next day either. Not wanting to disappoint Kelly, Spenser resumed his search early in the morning.

The horse had strayed over into the town limits of Culver and was near the structure Spenser had used for concealment. He had just found the mare when he spotted Mendez crouched behind the cactus.

Thinking the behavior odd and too far away to make out Mendez's features, Spenser had watched as Mendez knocked out two men before shooting two others.

Using his camera, Spenser zoomed in on the scene and was able to see that the man doing the killing was a cop, as the gold badge on Mendez's hip glittered in the sunlight. He had brought the digital camera along to aid in his search for Kelly's horse. By using the zoom function, he was able to cover a greater area by traveling a lesser distance.

Spenser had captured the shootings in detail with his camera, although he was too distant to clearly identify the wording on Mendez's badge. Still, if a cop were only wearing a badge and no uniform, it signified that he was a chief of police, or perhaps a detective.

Spenser was neither appalled or unapproving of the cop's actions. The men he killed were engaged in making meth. Spenser recognized the scent that the manufacturing of the drug produced and had smelled the sweet ether odor in the air before locating the horse.

Whoever the cop was, he was willing to do what needed to be done. Spenser would have acted no differently. If the cop hadn't killed the death merchants, Spenser may have returned someday with Cody and done the deed.

Stark was going to be Cody's home again. There was no way he would have allowed a group of meth dealers to ruin his town with their insidious product. Whoever the cop was, Spenser applauded his actions.

~

SARA ARRIVED BACK IN STARK AND FELT THE DIFFERENCE IN climate, as it was much warmer than New York City had been, where summer temperatures had yet to settle in. The storm of the previous evening had made the air less humid, which was welcome. The rain was appreciated, as the area had suffered an extended period of drought over the last twenty-two years. It had changed the land and made raising cattle unsustainable.

Cody wanted to breed cattle again, although he was willing to settle on raising horses if he had to. If the rain continued to increase and the land revived, he might get his wish, and the Parkers would once again raise cattle. Sara smiled, being the wife of a rancher was not something she had ever envisioned for herself, but she had taken to the ranch and loved the land, the space, the sense of freedom. She may have been born and bred in Connecticut and had a love of New York City, but they were not places where she wanted to raise a family.

Cody, as a Parker, had land and a legacy. Their children would benefit from both of those and on their trips to the city gain a sophistication that many rural inhabitants might never enjoy. In other words, they would have the best of both worlds.

Spenser came out to greet Sara as she arrived home from the airport. He had just gotten back to the ranch himself, after returning Kelly's horse to her. The little girl was thrilled to have the mare, Princess, back, and had thanked Spenser for finding her.

Sara had been unaware of Doc's close call of the day before. After carrying Sara's bags into the house and settling in the living room to talk, Sara was enthralled as Spenser told her of Doc's bravery in saving Kelly.

"It nearly cost him his life though."

"Thank God you followed him, Spenser. That sweet old man is like a part of the family, and it would have been horrible for Kelly to live with the fact that her grandfather died while saving her."

"Some good came out of it. Doc's daughter is speaking to him again."

"That's great. At his age, he should have his loved ones around him."

"He's not alone there. I've been moping around my home ever since Amy left me. Being here and being useful has revived my spirit, and to see Cody so happy, I can't tell you how pleased that makes me, Sara. You're the best thing that ever happened to Cody and I can't wait to see you two marry."

Sara stretched up and kissed Spenser on his bearded cheek. "Thank you, and I guess you'll be my father-in-law."

Spenser laughed. "I hadn't thought of it that way, but yes, Cody is like a son to me. I love that boy, and I'm proud of him. Not only is he building a life, he's rebuilding one. What he's doing takes a lot of guts. Coming back to reclaim his name could have become a disaster, but he'll pull it off."

"Thanks to you and Romeo."

"About that, I believe you have something for me."

"You're right," Sara said. She walked over to one of her suitcases, rummaged around in it, and returned to the sofa a few moments later. When she handed Spenser the item she had taken from the bag, he grinned at it.

"I don't know how that boy comes up with his plans, but he's outdone himself with this one. When do we have to put on our show?"

"Sometime tonight, or maybe even tomorrow. Cody will call when it's time."

"This is going to work, Sara."

"Yes, although I'm still nervous about something going wrong."

"How did your interview with Blue Truth go?"

"It went well, and Cody said that the woman who interviewed me made contact with the marshal I directed her to. This whole thing only works because of Thomas Lawson. I wish the man was coming to the wedding."

"What's Lawson like?"

"He seems average, but he wields great influence in Washington. When this is over, Tanner will be carrying out a contract for the man, as thanks."

"Who is the target?"

"Cody doesn't know yet, but they won't be a saint. Thomas Lawson tends to pick targets that deserve death. You don't need to be concerned that he'll send Tanner after a political target or an innocent."

"If that happened, Tanner would refuse to take the contract; I taught Cody better than that."

Sara gave a little laugh. "Listen to us. We keep switching back and forth between referring to him as Cody and Tanner."

"They're the same man, and yet, he's definitely Cody when he's here."

"He's not here now, he's in New York, and so is Tanner."

"And the so-called Magic Man is going to wish he'd never heard of him."

23

GOT YA!

NEW YORK CITY

AFTER THE MAGIC MAN TOLD DWIGHT HIS PLANS FOR
Tanner, Dwight volunteered to put it into action. Baxter
was reluctant to agree at first, until Dwight appealed to his
massive ego.

"Nothing will go wrong since it's your plan. You've
figured out a way to turn Tanner's strength into a weakness
and now I just have to spring your trap."

"That's true."

"Let me do it, Jonathon. That way I'll get credit for
killing Tanner too."

Baxter agreed and Dwight went into action. He had to
visit three stores to get the needed supplies, then he went to
work on the abandoned fire-ravaged home in Harlem.
Before starting, he stuck a sign out front that he had stolen
off the lawn of another home. The sign had the name of a
company that did home renovations. With his tool belt on

and a hard hat on his head, Dwight looked as if he belonged inside the building.

He figured he'd have to work deep into the night to get everything done. When it was finished, the trap would be set, and Tanner would be lured into it. Dwight had faith in Baxter's plan and the thought that it wouldn't succeed never entered his mind. After all, Jonathon Baxter was the Magic Man, and the Magic Man never failed.

In California, a nervous Caleb waited inside a restaurant for his date to arrive. Jen had been busy catching up with family and friends on her visit home but had agreed to have dinner with Caleb at a popular seafood restaurant.

Caleb wondered what his brother would think if he knew he was dating the doctor. It was a huge risk to do so, but since Jen had stumbled across him on the plane, Caleb didn't want to waste the opportunity to see her again. He liked Jen and felt good when he was around her. He hadn't gone out with anyone in months and it had been over three years since his last relationship ended. If tonight was the beginning of something more than a friendship, so be it. Although, being Stark would complicate things.

Jen arrived wearing a blue dress that flaunted her shapely legs. The woman was not only smart, talented, and had a good sense of humor, but she made Caleb's pulse race whenever he was near her.

"You look fantastic," Caleb told her, as she greeted him with a kiss on the cheek.

"You too, and I like your sports coat."

"It's new. I wanted to impress you."

Jen laughed. "Mission accomplished."

As the waiter came over to the table to take Jen's drink order, the date got underway. Although Jen and Caleb didn't know it, they were being observed.

~

FBI AGENT AMANDA ERIKSEN WAS OUTSIDE THE restaurant sitting in her personal vehicle. Eriksen was on the last day of her three day break and had spent the time following Jen around. After two days of watching the woman interact with friends and family, Eriksen was beginning to think she was wasting her time. Tonight though, as she looked through the zoom lens of her camera, she was wondering if she were gazing at Stark.

He would be about the right age and height that Stark has been described as being, she thought, as she scrutinized Caleb. It also did not escape her notice that the man was handsome.

Eriksen knew from talking to the doctor that first time in a Texas hospital that she held affection for Stark. When the doctor appeared anxious about the man who had dropped her off at home the other day, Eriksen decided to play a hunch.

The young man inside the restaurant might only be a friend of Jennifer Mao. However, the way the two were interacting with each other seemed like first date jitters to Eriksen, who was a trained observer of people.

If the man was Stark, it was foolish of him to seek a relationship with a stranger, even if he had saved the woman's life. Dr. Jennifer Mao was a true beauty; Stark wouldn't be the first man to have lust be his downfall.

After getting enough pictures of Caleb, Eriksen began looking up and down the street at the vehicles parked nearby. When she spotted the black pickup truck she had seen outside the doctor's home days earlier, she took down its license plate number.

When she returned to work, she would run the plate and have the subject's name and other information. If the man wooing Dr. Jen Mao was Stark, his days of freedom were numbered.

24
READY... SET...

CHICAGO

Romeo had stayed overnight in the Second City. He had arrived the day before, hours after killing Fontaine in New York. He had a new target, and his name was Harkness. Jared Harkness was the reason the Magic Man and his hitters were targeting Tanner in the first place. Romeo thought it would be a pleasure to put the man down.

He had followed Harkness for a day to see where he would go and record his movements. Harkness had gone to the office building where Ordnance Inc. had their headquarters, although the name on the directory in the lobby stated that it was the home offices of a corporation named Solution Allies.

Later, Romeo watched as Harkness met a woman in a bar and took her back to his hotel room. Romeo spent the night in another hotel a block away, then rose early to get ready for the day. After a hard run at sunrise along

Chicago's Lakefront Trail, Romeo showered and returned to Harkness's hotel.

Harkness left the hotel early with the woman from the bar on his arm as they went out to have breakfast.

As he was heading up to Harkness's hotel room, Romeo removed the electronic device he carried in a pocket and studied it. It appeared to be a hotel key card but was actually a sophisticated electronic lock pick.

After swiping it through the lock on Harkness's door, the device went to work deciphering the info needed to open it. When Romeo swiped the card through the lock a second time, it disengaged, and he gained entrance to Harkness's suite. The device had been supplied to Romeo by Duke, and the king of the black-market had just gained another client.

Once inside the room, Romeo went through Harkness's belongings as he searched for anything of value or interest. He found nothing, then went to work setting up the hidden camera he had brought along with him. The camera was designed to fit over an electrical outlet and blend in. It had a wide-angle lens, was capable of transmitting sound, and would send an alert to his phone whenever motion activated it.

Romeo used his gloved fingers to attach the device to the wall that faced the doorway. When he was done checking his phone to see if it worked properly, he left the hotel to visit the coffee shop across the street.

After taking a table that gave him a good view of the entrance to the hotel, Romeo ordered breakfast. As he ate, he read a book. If Harkness returned, the camera would let him know.

～

BACK IN NEW YORK CITY, DWIGHT RUBBED THE BACK OF his neck as he looked over his handiwork. He had spent most of the previous night setting a trap for Tanner. The Magic Man had figured out Tanner's greatest strength. It was the fact that the man was devious and did the unexpected. Those same attributes could be used against Tanner by anticipating them. On the top floor of the three-story home was a room where Dwight had placed a chair. The fire that had forced the building's occupants to flee had been located on the other side of the home. Other than the scent of smoke, this side of the house was untouched.

There were three options to reach the room with the chair in it, since it had connecting doors to two other rooms. You had to travel up the stairs and then walk down a hallway to reach any of the rooms. Dwight had spent the night rigging the house. If you didn't approach the room on one undeviating route, you would meet your death. The Magic Man's logic was simple. Since Tanner never came at you directly, make all indirect paths to his target death traps.

Dwight had sawn through floorboards inside the rooms that connected to the target room and had removed sections of the floor or ceiling beneath them. Afterward, he had covered the holes again with the loose cut pieces. At a glance, the floor looked all right, although it would collapse if walked upon.

Anyone falling through the floor would plummet about twenty feet. Their landing would be a rough one, thanks to the large spikes sticking up from the floor below.

Dwight was to follow Tanner until he was spotted, then make a run for the house, enter the room with the chair, and wait. When Tanner attempted to sneak up on his target's location, as the Magic Man was certain he would, the hit man would suffer a fall and be skewered.

Dwight didn't know if he'd be willing to finish Tanner off, but he would have no problem letting the man suffer until he died. The only misery Dwight had ever cared about was his own.

Work had also been performed on the exterior of the home with booby traps devised by the Magic Man. If Tanner attempted to enter the target room through a window, he would die just as surely.

Dwight double-checked everything before leaving the house. He was tired and aching from the unaccustomed physical labor, but he felt good. Tanner, the man whom so many had died trying to kill was going to finally get his. When everyone asked who had killed him, Dwight's name would be mentioned alongside that of the Magic Man. Their reputations would skyrocket, and they would be able to triple what they were charging.

As he walked down the block to get in his car and drive to his hotel, Dwight thought of all the things he would buy with the money he would make off his new rep. He never once noticed that Tanner was watching him from across the street.

TANNER HAD FOLLOWED DWIGHT FROM THE HOTEL WHERE Fontaine said the man was staying. He had been trailing behind him as he shopped for tools and supplies for the work he'd had ahead of him. When Dwight began working on the house, Tanner wasn't sure what to make of it, but after hearing the power saw cutting through wood, he understood—Dwight was building a trap.

Tanner went home to the penthouse around midnight,

where he slept a full night's sleep. When he arrived back at the house in Harlem at eight the next morning, Dwight was just finishing up.

Tanner wasn't certain what Dwight had been doing, but he knew one thing, he was never going to enter that house.

He followed Dwight to the hotel and watched him get on the elevator. Having been up all night, the Magic Man's flunky would get a few hours' rest. Tanner never considered breaking into Dwight's hotel room and killing him. No, he had other plans for Dwight. After taking out his phone, Tanner typed a text message to Romeo and Spenser.

SHOW TIME WILL TAKE PLACE LATER TODAY. STAY READY!

BOTH MEN ANSWERED HIM WITHIN SECONDS, AND TANNER decided to leave Dwight and go have breakfast somewhere. Dwight didn't know it, but he was about to become a pawn in a drama that Tanner was putting on for Blue Truth's benefit. If it worked, the authorities would never connect him with Tanner, and Cody Parker could live life without fear of exposure.

Of course, even if everything went perfectly, Ordnance Inc. was still in the wings.

One thing at a time, Tanner told himself. *One thing at a time.*

IN CHICAGO, TREVOR HEALY WAS SURPRISED TO FIND HIS boss, Grayson Talbot, in the office so early. For that matter,

Grayson hadn't been around much at all. Ordnance Inc. had grown rapidly, and Grayson had decided to open a second office to work out of. That was fine by Healy, as he preferred to run things without anyone hovering over him.

After exchanging greetings, they settled together in Talbot's office, which was larger still than Healy's grand office suite.

"How are things going at the new location, Grayson?"

"Have a seat, Trevor."

When he saw the scowl on Grayson's face, Healy knew criticism was coming his way.

"What's going on with you and Jared Harkness?"

"We discussed it last week, when I told you about Tanner's phone call."

"You placated the hit man by refusing to help Jared?"

"Yes."

"Then why was Jared in the building recently?"

Healy cleared his throat. He should have known better than to think he could keep something hidden from Talbot. The opposite wasn't true. Talbot had changed over the last year. His obsession with work and his micro-management style had lessened as he had piled more responsibility onto Healy. There were personal changes as well. Talbot once wore the same thing every day, as if the clothes were a uniform. Now, he could often be seen in a suit or casual attire. His present mood aside, Talbot had seemed happier as well recently. If Healy didn't believe the man was incapable of it, he might have guessed that Talbot had fallen in love.

After wetting his lips with his tongue, Healy explained. "I saw an opportunity and I acted on it."

"Explain that?"

"I introduced Jared to one of the outside contractors we sometimes use, the Magic Man."

"By doing that, you've involved us with Jared again. What do you think would happen if Tanner could prove a connection?"

Healy raised up a hand, as if pleading for understanding. "I know it was risky, but the Magic Man has never failed. If anyone could come up with a plan to kill Tanner, it would be him."

Talbot slammed a palm against his desktop. "I have a plan to kill Tanner, and we've spent a year putting it into action. Now you tell me that you may have placed everything at risk?"

Healy felt himself growing angry and decided not to fight it. He leaned forward in his seat.

"What risk, Grayson? If Tanner dared to attack us, we'd have the manpower to deal with him. We could send over a dozen Hammer teams against the man now. He would never survive that."

"Let's say you're right, that still doesn't mean he might not begin his attack by murdering the two of us."

Healy fell back in his seat. "That's true, and he'd start with me. The man warned me that if we ever came at him again, I would die."

The room fell silent for several moments, then Grayson spoke.

"What's the status concerning the Magic Man?"

Healy brightened. "I spoke with Jared yesterday; the Magic Man assured him that Tanner would be dead by the end of today."

"Let's hope so. If not, *we* may be dead by the end of the day."

"I'm sorry, Grayson."

"You made a decision, but Trevor, let's stick to the original plan. We're months away from being ready to implement it."

"I believe we're ready now."

"I want to be more than prepared. I don't intend to underestimate Tanner a second time."

Healy nodded. "As you wish, but I'm not good at being patient."

"Trust me, Trevor, when we do strike, revenge will be ten times sweeter."

"And there's always the chance that the Magic Man will succeed."

Talbot smiled. "Now that would be some real magic."

GO!

NEW YORK CITY

AFTER CATCHING A FEW HOURS OF SLEEP, DWIGHT ROSE, showered, and went out for a bite to eat. He was stiff with muscle ache from the work he had done overnight. That aside, he felt good, and was ravenous. Once he finished his meal, he was going to spend the rest of the day outside the building where Tanner lived. When the hit man appeared, Dwight would put the Magic Man's scheme in motion by luring Tanner to the property.

What Dwight didn't know is that while he was asleep, Tanner had anonymously tipped off the city about the booby-trapped building. Engineers from New York's building department had cordoned off the fire damaged structure and were examining the damage.

There was a coffee shop near his hotel. Dwight walked there, then settled at a small table where he could be alone to play a game on his phone. When the waitress asked him what he wanted, Dwight ordered a feast.

Outside the coffee shop, Tanner took out his phone and sent off two text messages. One was sent to Spenser and the other to Romeo. They contained one word—Go!

In Stark, Spenser climbed behind the wheel of a pickup truck as Sara got in the passenger seat. When she looked over at Spenser, she shook her head in wonderment.

"I still can't believe how real those masks look; if I didn't know differently, I'd think I was sitting next to Cody."

"I'll go you one better," Spenser said, then he proceeded to speak in an excellent imitation of Cody's voice.

"Okay, now that's spooky," Sara said.

Spenser spoke in his own voice again. "I'll only do that if we get cornered by someone that knows Cody."

"We shouldn't if you stay in the truck and let me run interference, but we need for him to be seen in Stark, in case there's a question about his whereabouts later."

Spenser started up the truck. "Let's go be seen."

In Chicago, Romeo, who was also wearing a Tanner mask, took the elevator up to the floor where Harkness's suite was located. Harkness had returned earlier, and Romeo had sent off a text telling Tanner that he was ready when he was. That time had arrived, and Harkness would learn what so many had discovered before him: targeting

Tanner wasn't good for your health. Romeo knocked on the hotel room door and announced that he was from the front desk.

"I have a package for you, sir."

"Hold on," came the voice from behind the door. To avoid having Harkness see his face, Romeo turned his back to the peephole and pretended like he was talking to another of the hotel's guest. He was in a one-sided conversation about sheets. Meanwhile, he was looking at his phone screen, to observe Harkness through the hidden camera he'd concealed inside the room earlier.

When the door behind him opened, Romeo turned and pushed into the room while filling his hand with a gun. He was armed with a PSS, a silent pistol. The door slammed into Harkness and sent him stumbling backwards.

"What the hell?"

Romeo was firing his gun before Harkness could utter another word. He shot Jared Harkness three times in the chest before placing a round in his head. The sound of the body hitting the floor made far more noise than the shots had.

After reclaiming the hidden camera he'd placed inside earlier, Romeo left the hotel room at a run as he headed for the stairs. There were cameras inside the hotel's corridors, and so there was a chance that a security guard had watched Romeo shove his way into the room. However, there were no cameras in the stairwell, that was why Romeo made a point of taking off the Tanner mask he was wearing while he was still in view of a camera. He did so while obscuring his true face, but his long blond hair was visible.

After entering the stairwell, Romeo tucked the mask inside his shirt while also removing a cap from it. With his hair tucked up inside the cap, he stripped off his jacket and turned it inside out. The garment was reversible, making the green jacket the shooter wore turn into a red one. The top sections from a pair of white canvas sneakers had been glued in place over the black rubber-soled shoes Romeo wore. He removed the camouflage material and stuffed them inside the jacket's pockets.

Sprinting down the stairs, Romeo went three flights before entering a hallway and heading for an elevator, as he passed a maid, he reported to her that there was a man in the stairwell acting strange.

"What's he look like, sir?"

"He's wearing a green jacket and sneakers, and there's blood on his pantleg."

The maid, who was also a supervisor, took out her phone and called security. By their response, Romeo became certain that no one had viewed him pushing in Harkness's door. After telling the maid that he was in a hurry to get to a meeting, Romeo got on an elevator and took it to the lobby, A minute later he was on the street and in the clear.

BACK IN STARK, SARA WAS WAVING HELLO TO BETH AND Kelly as Spenser drove past the veterinarian's office with his Tanner mask on. At the corner he made a left turn and headed toward the town's municipal center. There were several cops standing outside the building. Spenser pulled to the curb and Sara got out of the truck to walk over to a mailbox and send off a letter.

As she was getting back inside the vehicle, a voice called out. "Hey there, Cody, Sara."

Spenser turned his head to look and saw Chief

Mendez walking toward them. He had observed the man in the side-view mirror before the chief spoke. Now it appeared that Mendez was in the mood to chat. Spenser waved at the chief but remained silent.

Sara spoke to the chief. "We can't stay and talk, Chief, we're late for a meeting with the caterer."

"That's more important, so I'll see you two around."

Spenser waved again, then drove the truck away slowly.

"That was close," Sara said.

"I might have pulled it off."

"Not if he started talking about the old days; he was Cody's best friend back then."

"I remember. I met him briefly once. He struck me as being a tough kid in those days. He's become an even tougher adult."

"What do you mean?"

"Just a hunch," Spenser said.

"I think we've done our part; let's head back to the ranch."

"Only after we make a stop at the caterer you're using, in case the chief verifies your story."

"Why would he?"

"I don't know, but if he does, you'll be covered. Just go inside the office and double-check that they're prepared for the wedding; it will calm your nerves anyway."

Sara grinned. "I am nervous, but it's a good nervous, like excitement."

"I can tell, and in his own way, I'm sure that Cody is feeling the same thing."

"Thank you again for helping us, Spenser."

"No need to thank me; we're family, Sara, or we will be when you marry Cody."

Sara gazed out the side window of the truck. "I hope everything goes well on his end."

"Tanner can handle anything," Spenser said.

~

IN NEW YORK CITY, DWIGHT WAS FINISHING UP A HUGE breakfast that had consisted of a three-egg omelet, bacon, French toast, and a vanilla milkshake. He was stuffed and felt like he wanted to go back to his room and sleep another few hours. He couldn't do that, of course, for it was time to find Tanner and set the trap.

As Tanner's name was going through his mind, Dwight looked up to see the man walking into the restaurant. He blinked, while thinking he was imagining things. He blinked a second time in astonishment, as Tanner's right hand moved in a blur of motion to draw a gun from a hip holster.

"No! Don't!" Dwight said.

Tanner ignored him and sent six rounds into Dwight. Contrary to the Magic Man's belief, there were times when Tanner came straight at a target. This was one of those times. It needed to be one of those times, and it required an audience as well.

The other patrons in the restaurant either ran out in panic while screaming or ducked down beneath their tables. Tanner leapt over the counter to land beside a waitress, then rushed toward the rear of the business.

The guy handling the grill brandished a meat cleaver, but Tanner was past him before the man could become a threat. Once he was in the narrow alleyway at the rear of the street's line of shops, Tanner rushed down it to reach the avenue on the other side of the block.

Sirens were already growing closer and the police would be blocking the alley off at any moment. There may not be a cop around when you needed one, but they damn well made an appearance when you didn't want one. With over thirty-eight thousand cops on the force in New York City, the odds were good that a uniformed officer wasn't far away from where Tanner was.

There was a camera situated above the door that was the rear entrance of a jewelry shop. Its blinking red light told Tanner that it was on.

With the siren growing louder, Tanner stripped off the mask of his own face that he was wearing. After tossing it aside, he made certain to let the camera capture the face that was beneath the mask. It was yet another mask, and it was the face of Trevor Healy. Lisa had done a rush job on the Healy mask. The face was right, but he had Tanner's hair.

Tanner left the alley, bought a paper from a vendor, then leaned back against a parked car as if he were waiting for someone.

A cop on foot came around the corner an instant later, as a police car crept into the alley from the other end. The cop who was running came to a skidding halt after spotting the mask. After taking out a latex glove, the officer picked up the Tanner mask, then rushed to catch up to the cops inside the patrol car.

Tanner walked across the street, hailed a taxi, and while talking with the Healy mask on, he told the man to take him to the airport. He had a jet to catch to Seattle.

26

SEE YOURSELF ON TV

IN NEW YORK CITY, VICTOR MIDDLETON BEGAN A meeting between himself, Derek Warner, and Sofia Diaz. A man named Jared Harkness was murdered hours earlier inside his Chicago hotel room by an assassin whose features resembled the image on the flyer of Tanner. A security camera captured the man doing something to his face, like possibly removing a mask. At the very least it was a dark wig and revealed that the hair beneath it was blond. The camera did not record his true features.

Dwight's murder and the video that captured it, had also come to Blue Truth's attention. Seeing the killer strip off the mask was a shock, as was the recovery of the disguise the same assassin wore in New York.

Victor summed things up. "I was only allowed to view the mask in an evidence bag, but it looks like the descriptions of Tanner that we've all heard about. Not only that but the murder here and the murder in Chicago took place only minutes apart. I think there's no doubt anymore that Tanner is not one single man."

"Then, what exactly do we have here, some kind of murderous gang?" Sofia asked.

"I don't think it's that organized," Victor said. "As for the masks, there's probably someone on the black-market cashing in by supplying them to hired killers. Want to increase your fee? Call yourself Tanner, you know, that sort of thing."

Derek raised a hand in objection. "Hold up. We know the guy here in New York was wearing a mask, but that doesn't mean the man in Chicago was wearing one too."

"He removed a mask, Derek, you saw the video," Sofia said.

"He took off something, a wig for sure, but since we never got a look at his face afterward, there's no way to be certain."

"What are you saying, that he just happened to look like the other man, only he was really blond?"

"No, Victor, but do we know where this guy Cody Parker was yesterday? Maybe he was in Chicago wearing two different wigs to confuse things."

"He has a point, Victor," Sofia said. "Can we verify Mr. Parker's whereabouts when these two homicides were taking place?"

Victor looked confused. "He can't be an assassin. The man spent more than twenty years inside the WITSEC program."

"True, Parker was in witness protection, that's been verified, but it doesn't hurt to check all the bases," Sofia said.

"Where is Mr. Parker living these days?"

"He's in a Texas town called Stark," Sofia said.

Derek's eyes lit up in recognition. "Stark, Texas? I know the man who's the chief of police there. He's a former DEA agent named Mendez. I'll give him a call; the man's a friend."

"Do that, if you want," Victor said, "but I doubt Chief Mendez will say he can prove Cody Parker was in Chicago yesterday. I'm declaring the Tanner myth a dead case. I want to move on to something else."

"I'll second that," Sofia said.

"Yeah, I agree, but I'll still give Steve Mendez a call," Derek said.

"We'll place a short post on the website stating that the existence of a super assassin named Tanner is just a myth."

"It won't matter, Victor," Sofia said. "People will still tell stories about him and give him credit for assassinations. The guys running around in the masks will keep the myth alive."

"Speaking of assassinations, have you two heard about this dude they're calling the Magic Man?" Derek asked.

Sofia laughed. "The Magic Man? Are you joking?"

"That's what they call him. He's supposed to be some sort of criminal mastermind who plans out assassinations for contract killers."

Sofia waved a hand in a dismissive gesture. "One assassin was enough; I want to investigate something else, something different."

"Like what?" Derek asked.

Sofia grinned. "Bigfoot."

~

SEATTLE, WASHINGTON

TANNER HAD FLOWN ON A CITATION X IN ORDER TO REACH Seattle as quickly as possible. He didn't want to give the

Magic Man time to become worried and go off somewhere to hide. Despite that, the trip still took four hours. By the time he had claimed his rented car—obtained under a throwaway ID—and arrived at Jonathon Baxter's house, nearly another hour had gone by.

∾

BAXTER WAS WORRIED. HE HADN'T HAD ANY WORD FROM Dwight other than a text that Dwight had sent him that morning.

THE TRAP IS SET. I'LL BE LURING THE MOUSE INTO IT SOON.

BAXTER RELEASED A SIGH. *DWIGHT COULD BE DEAD.* THE sigh and the thought were followed by a laugh. *No, in order for Dwight to be dead, I would have had to of been wrong about Tanner. I was not wrong.*

Baxter was in his back yard again, while tending to his flowers. He had removed a row of hedges earlier in order to plant more roses. The work had tired him, and he had taken a break to have a beer and fry up a hamburger on the grill.

With his meal eaten and the beer consumed, he went back to preparing the ground for the roses. When he had the soil the way he wanted it, he began inserting the plants into it, as he positioned the second one, a voice spoke from behind him.

"You're planting them too closely together."

Baxter turned around to look at his visitor. He had never seen a photo of Tanner but had heard that the man had an intense gaze. That descriptor was an understatement; Baxter found he had trouble keeping eye contact.

"Who… who are you?"

"My name is Tanner, and you call yourself the Magic Man."

Baxter was about to deny knowing what Tanner was talking about when Tanner gave him the news.

"Your man Dwight is dead. I shot him in New York City about five hours ago."

Baxter couldn't help it. He had to ask. "How did you do it? Did you sneak up on him?"

Tanner answered while grabbing the shovel Baxter had used earlier.

"I walked straight up to him inside a restaurant and fired six slugs into him."

"Listen, Tanner, we can make a deal. I can always find work for an assassin like yourself. Why don't we form an alliance?"

"I prefer to freelance," Tanner said. He raised the shovel and brought it down with such speed that the Magic Man couldn't utter a cry of alarm. The first blow stunned him, while the fifth killed him.

Tanner left the home some time later, after planting the roses. The Magic Man was in the ground beneath them and would act as fertilizer. What was left of his remains wouldn't be discovered for many decades.

Two hours later, Cody was on another flight. His wedding day was approaching fast, and he was headed home, home to the ranch, and the woman he loved.

Before leaving Chicago, Romeo performed a final errand, as he dropped off an envelope at the reception area of a company called Solution Allies, or as some knew them, Ordnance Inc.

The envelope contained a letter that had been written by Tanner, although, he'd left it unsigned. When Healy opened it at his desk, he had no doubt who had sent it.

Our truce still stands, because I can't prove that you were behind the Magic Man's attempts to kill me. Harkness is dead and the Magic Man has performed a disappearing act.

Healy, if you try something like this again, you'll join them, and proof be damned.

Later that night, while watching the news, Trevor Healy saw video that had been filmed by a security camera. It showed a man who looked like Tanner stripping off a mask to reveal Healy's own face. The report stated that the suspect who resembled Healy was wanted for murdering a man named Dwight Wheatley.

"That son of a bitch," Healy muttered, before turning off the TV.

27

THE THINGS WE DO FOR LOVE

TANNER FLEW OUT OF SEATTLE AND CODY PARKER returned to the ranch in the early morning hours. It was raining again in Stark, and the cars parked near the house glistened under the floodlights that came on at Cody's approach. Despite the late hour, Sara greeted him at the front door. Her beaming face and welcoming embrace made Cody glad that she had waited up for him.

After a kiss of greeting, Cody slipped off his damp jacket and they moved into the kitchen, where Sara had been sipping on a cup of tea. As Cody settled beside her at the table, Sara slid a computer tablet over to him. On its screen was the home page of Blue Truth's website. There was a proclamation on the findings of their latest investigation.

THE ELITE ASSASSIN NAMED TANNER IS A MYTH; Killers Don Mask To Fake The Boogeyman Of The Underworld.

. . .

TANNER NODDED WITH SATISFACTION AT THE STORY, surprising Sara by his lack of enthusiasm that his plan had worked so well.

"What's wrong? I thought you'd be happier about this. Everything went the way you planned."

"I am happy; this means we don't have to be concerned that the law will bother us, but it does have a downside too."

"A downside?" Sara said, while staring at the words on the website. When the truth struck her, she brought her hand to her mouth. "Oh my God, Cody, I see what you mean. By doing this... you've destroyed your reputation. People will read this and believe it and... no one will want to contract with Tanner, not if they believe he's a myth."

"It's a temporary situation, Sara. In time, Tanner will be recognized again. I'll see to that."

Sara caressed his cheek. "You sacrificed yourself, yourself as Tanner so that Cody Parker could live again. You did this for me?"

"I did it for us, and for the children we'll have someday. Let everyone think that Tanner is a myth and let him stay a myth for a while. In the meantime, Cody Parker is going to build a life. Romeo said something to me once a long time ago that's stuck with me. He said that being an assassin was an adventure, not a life, and that when he was an old man, he wanted to have his family around him. I want a life too, Sara; I want a life with you."

They left the kitchen and headed up to their bedroom, while walking hand in hand.

SUSPICIOUS MINDS

CALIFORNIA

THE FOLLOWING MORNING, AGENT AMANDA ERIKSEN WAS at her desk reading a file she had requested. It concerned Caleb Knox.

Eriksen was surprised to learn that Caleb was the adoptive son of John Knox, the highly decorated police officer. She remembered hearing that John Knox had died recently.

As for Caleb, Eriksen found herself feeling sympathy for the man after reading about his early years. Caleb's mother had been taken from her home and family by her demented brother, Billy Gant, when she was carrying Caleb. Gant was the son of the crazed deceased doomsday cult leader, William Gant.

During his formative years, Caleb must have observed Billy Gant and his gang of thieves and mercenaries rob countless people. The boy could have grown up to be like them, or to despise them. In a way, he had done both. By becoming a thief who stole from other thieves, Caleb Knox acted as a vigilante.

Although she had no solid evidence that Caleb was indeed Stark, Eriksen knew in her bones that he was her man. During the period she had spent following Jen around, Eriksen had much time to think. Although she felt compassion for Caleb concerning his past, she still planned to see the man behind bars someday. Despite that, an idea had occurred to her.

As Stark, Caleb Knox was attempting to form a working relationship with her, so that they could help each other. As much as she didn't like to admit it, the man was useful and had a knack for hunting down thieves.

So, why not leave him out there and benefit from him? Now that she knew who he was, she could track Stark and use him as a sort of stalking horse for other criminals. If the man was so gung-ho to help her, Eriksen would let him, then, when she felt the time was right, she'd slap the cuffs on Caleb.

Eriksen smiled as she imagined the look that would be on Stark's face when that day arrived.

WHEN HE WAS ALONE IN HIS OFFICE WITH THE DOOR SHUT, Derek Warner removed a cell phone from a locked drawer in his desk. The phone's battery was low but still had enough charge to make a call. After looking up a number, Derek pushed a button.

WHEN CHIEF MENDEZ FELT HIS SECOND CELL PHONE vibrate in his pocket, he took it out while rolling up the windows of his vehicle. He was seated in the parking lot of the Stark Diner while he read over recent crime statistics on a laptop computer.

The second cell phone only rang when another member of the group he was involved with wanted to talk. The rumors about a secret faction of vigilantes within law enforcement that Tamir Ivanov told Pullo about were true. Mendez was a member, as was Derek Warner. They called themselves Sword Bearers.

When he answered the phone, Mendez did so while uttering two words. "Lady justice?"

"Holds a sword to carry out punishment. Hey, Steve, this is Derek Warner."

"Derek, hey pardner, how's it going? I heard you were making fat money working for that think tank."

"It pays better than Uncle Sam, and it's the reason I'm calling."

"What's up?"

"Do you know a guy in that two-horse town of yours named Cody Parker?"

Mendez had been sitting relaxed after hearing Derek's voice; at the mention of Cody's name he sat up straight in his seat.

"I know Parker, what about him?"

"When was the last time you saw him?"

"Yesterday, he and his fiancée were out and about, and I spotted Cody as his wife-to-be was mailing a letter."

"That would be Sara Blake. She's an ex-FBI agent."

"Now that I didn't know."

"And you're certain it was yesterday that you saw Parker?"

"I'm positive."

"What time was it?"

When Mendez told Derek the time, he heard a sigh come over the phone.

"Well, that settles that."

"Settles what, Derek?"

"This guy Parker is the spitting image of the assassin named Tanner."

"Tanner? The hit man Tanner? Cody?"

Derek's laugh was derisive. "I know, right? The dude hid out inside the WITSEC program for most of his life. A wimp like that couldn't be Tanner, in fact, there is no Tanner, not really."

Mendez leaned back in his seat, his interest piqued. "Tell me all about it, Derek."

BY THE TIME MENDEZ ENDED THE CALL, HE HAD HEARD THE details of Blue Truth's investigation into the Tanner legend. He checked his email for the video Derek said he would forward to him. It was the video that had been taken inside the coffee shop in New York City where Tanner had killed Dwight; there was also the video of the killer removing a mask in an alleyway.

Mendez watched the videos three times each. "Damn but if that dude don't move like Cody," he said under his breath. After taking out his regular phone, Mendez called around until he found the caterer who was handling The Parker wedding.

"Yes, we're catering that affair, Chief."

"Can you tell me the last time you spoke to Sara Blake?"

"Sure, she was in here yesterday."

"It was yesterday, you're certain of that?"

"Mm-hmm, and we went over everything one last time… is there a problem, Chief?"

"No, ma'am, everything's fine, and you have a nice day now."

After the call, Mendez sat in his vehicle, while thinking about Cody, and an elite assassin named Tanner.

ALL SYSTEMS ARE GO

THE PARKER RANCH, STARK, TEXAS

Tanner was seated behind the desk in the home office at the ranch. He was calling Michael Barlow. When the man answered, he told Tanner that he was alone and able to talk.

The wedding was to take place the next day. Tanner wanted to learn if there was even a whiff in the air of an attack by Ordnance Inc.

"Kate and I have heard nothing that would indicate that, and besides, most of the Hammer teams are on their way to Mexico to handle the huge project going on there."

"What's that project about?"

"A player involved with a Mexican Cartel hired Ordnance Inc. to take out a business rival."

"Is the business related to drugs?"

"No, he's a legitimate businessman who's gathering support to run for office. The drug kingpin wants him dead because the man hates the cartels. This client is very wealthy. If the job is handled right, Healy thinks it could become a permanent gig and they'll be hired on as the client's personal army and be given the contract to provide protection."

"This drug kingpin, is he a man named Damián Sandoval?"

"No, I've never heard of him. The operation is taking place in Puebla, Mexico."

"What about Healy, has he mentioned my name when you were around him?"

"He's said nothing."

"All right, Barlow. If things change, call."

"Of course," Barlow said.

After disconnecting, Tanner made his next call.

Billy Price answered but was whispering. "I can't talk for long."

"I need to know if you've heard anything about there being plans to attack me."

"Hell, I would have called you."

"Good, Price, do that, call if you hear anything, even a rumor."

"You got it, Tanner."

As he put away the phone, Tanner's posture relaxed. He assumed that Ordnance Inc. was keeping track of him somehow. It would be an easy thing for them to send an operative to Stark to spy on him. He was the talk of the town since returning, after being presumed dead, hearing news of his upcoming wedding would be easy to learn. He had been concerned about an attack coming on their wedding day, fortunately, that fear seemed unfounded.

As he stood from the desk with his concerns gone, Tanner was again Cody and appeared to be at peace. After leaving the office he ran into Doc, who was working on replacing a damaged knob on a closet door.

"I thought you were told to take it easy for a while."

"It's just a doorknob, Cody; this won't take but a few minutes."

"Still, now that Sara and I will be living here full-time we'll be adding on more help. Your job will be to supervise the new people."

Doc grinned. "Do I get a raise?"

"Yeah, and a title if you want it. Not only did you bring me into the world, Doc, but you saved my life years ago when you dug a bullet out of me. If you asked me to, I'd give you a million dollars."

"I don't need charity, son, and I like keeping busy, but a little more money never hurts, especially now that I've got a granddaughter to spoil. How many people are you hiring?"

"Someone to help you around here, and I guess a housekeeper who can also cook. Once the ranch is up and running again, we'll be hiring hands too."

"You want to raise cattle? That's risky given the way the weather has been in recent years."

"I know, but I may give it a shot."

Spenser came down the hallway from his room holding a camera. He asked Cody if he could speak to him alone. After excusing themselves to Doc, they used the office and sat together on the sofa.

"What's up, Spenser?"

"It's about your friend, Chief Mendez," Spenser said, then he went on to tell Cody what he had witnessed in the desert. After speaking, he showed Cody the photos he'd taken of the events he had witnessed. "His features are a bit blurred because of the distance the photos were taken from, but I'm certain the man in the pictures is Chief Mendez. I found a photo of him online and compared it."

"It is, Spenser, and I see he's not shy about taking out the trash."

"The newspaper reported that it was done by a rival gang but doesn't name one."

"It's why Steve used three different guns, to make it seem that there were three different killers. If anyone cared enough, they might disprove that theory by studying the shoe prints, but I doubt there will be that level of an investigation for these dirtbags, and Steve would know that too."

"Yeah, and the sand out there is disturbed now from all the people who have visited the crime scene."

Cody handed back the camera. "Let me have copies of those; they may come in handy someday."

"To use it against the chief?"

"If he ever stumbles onto my being Tanner, it would help to have something to keep him from getting righteous and arresting me."

"I'm not sure he would, not a man who did what he did to those drug dealers. I'll say this for the chief, I believe he won't let crime get out of hand here."

Cody looked thoughtful. "I wonder if he killed the Harvey brothers too."

"Who were they?"

"The local drug dealers, until they were shot to death inside their truck a short time ago."

"I guess that's a possibility."

"Hmm, if so, that surprises me. Rich and Ernie were as low-level as drug dealers get. As far as I know, they never peddled the hard stuff."

"Maybe the ex-DEA agent Chief of Police has a low tolerance for drug dealing of any sort."

Cody stood up. "I have to take a ride out to the ranch's

landing field with Sara. Her father should be flying in soon. Do you want to come?"

"Yeah, and Romeo is at the airport picking up Nadya and Florentina; the big day is almost upon you, Cody."

"It feels like a miracle, Spenser. For years I lived as someone else and I never thought I'd get married; now I can't wait to settle down and be myself again, to live my life as Cody Parker."

"Tanner Three made it work, and you will too."

"There's still the threat of Ordnance Inc. to deal with, but they don't appear to be gunning for me right now. I'll handle them when I'm forced to. But the hell with them, I've a woman to marry, and a life to build."

"If the day comes when you have to fight them, Romeo and I will be at your side."

There was a knock on the door, then Sara stuck her head in. "Jenny called; Daddy will be landing in about twenty minutes."

"Let's go meet them," Cody said.

On his way out of the house, Cody grabbed a tan cowboy hat off an entry table and stuck it on his head.

"You were wearing a hat like that the first time I saw you," Spenser said.

"I grew up wearing them, and I always liked them too. I guess some of my old habits are returning to me now that I'm home."

Outside the house, decorations were being put up as the final preparations for the wedding were under way. Sara looked up at the cloudy sky with a worried frown.

"It better not rain tomorrow."

Cody kissed her. "It wouldn't dare."

30

MR. & MRS. CODY PARKER

THE PARKER RANCH, STARK, TEXAS

THE SKY CLEARED OVERNIGHT, AND A BRILLIANT DOME OF cloudless blue was the canopy for the wedding of Cody Parker and Sara Blake.

They were married by a retired judge who was the same man who had wed Cody's parents. The groom had donned a tux while the bride wore a traditional white wedding dress of delicate lace that fit her perfectly. Sara's hair was arranged in a swirl of dark curls that sat on her head like a crown.

After they were joined in matrimony, the couple kissed amid the cheers of their friends and family.

The guests were few, but all had deep ties to the couple and witnessed their joining. Among them was Caleb, who stood beside Romina Reyes. The two had met the day before and Romina took a liking to the handsome younger Parker brother. Although he flirted with Romina, Caleb found himself thinking about and missing Jennifer Mao.

Romeo was Cody's best man, and in that capacity, he had thrown Cody a bachelor party of sorts the night before. It consisted of himself, Spenser, and Cody sitting out on the porch and drinking champagne until after midnight. They weren't the sort of men who hired strippers, nor ones who had an assortment of acquaintances they counted as close companions. The three of them were more like family than friends, and they reminisced about the old days when they had traveled the Midwest together.

Joe Pullo hadn't arrived until early on the morning of the wedding, after sneaking out of New York City. Laurel enjoyed seeing Romina again, while Pullo was impressed by the size of the ranch. As a lifelong city dweller, the mob boss was used to much less open space.

CHIEF MENDEZ STOPPED BY DURING THE RECEPTION TO wish the couple luck. Cody spoke with him alone in the office for a few moments and brought up the subject of the dead meth dealers found in the desert.

"That happened over in Culver, but I got a look at the scene. It appeared as if they were taken out by three men."

"It sounds like someone did the town a favor. A meth epidemic is the last thing Stark needs."

"You're right about that, and as long as I'm chief, this town will be clean of drugs."

"It's a nicer place than it was when we were kids, thanks to all the money and jobs Chuck Willis brought to the area."

"Yeah, Willis is all right, and people are glad that you're back too. They're saying you're good luck, Cody."

"Why is that?"

"The rain. You may not know this, but the drought conditions around here started about the time your family was killed. And since you've been back, it's rained more than at any time in recent memory."

"Glad I could help."

"Ah, you joke, but it's true, and buddy, I'm glad you're back. Hell, man, I missed you something awful after thinking you were dead."

"I've thought of you over the years too, Steve."

Mendez held out his hand and Cody shook it. "Stop by the ranch again when we return from our honeymoon, and bring Ginny by too."

"I'll make a point of doing that," Mendez said.

Cody walked the chief out to the porch and watched him head down the stairs, as he was opening the door to go back inside the house, Mendez called to him.

"Yeah, Steve?"

"When you had come back here the first time, what name did you use?"

Cody stared at him a moment before answering. "Tanner, I called myself Tanner."

"Yeah, and wasn't that the name of the guy that was staying with your family back when the trouble happened?"

"That's right."

"That fella with the eye patch, Spenser? He reminds me of that guy."

"Yeah, there's a resemblance."

"I also hear tell that you got in a scuffle with the Harvey brothers on your first visit, Rich and Ernie. Folks say that cute gal Romina told everyone back then that you kicked their asses."

"Because of what happened to my family, I've learned to defend myself."

"A fellow I know called you a wimp, you know, because you sought shelter inside witness protection for so many years. Now me, I don't think you're a wimp at all, no sir, I do not."

"Sticks and stones," Cody said.

"Ha, that's right, who cares what people think?" Mendez smiled and waved. "I'll see you around, Cody."

"Goodbye, Steve."

This time, Cody watched Mendez until his vehicle disappeared around a curve in the driveway. Before going inside, he thought over the chief's words and decided that it was a good thing Spenser had given him ammunition to use against his old friend. Just in case, just in case.

31

THE REWARDS OF PATIENCE

As the wedding reception was going on in Texas, Michael and Kate Barlow were entertaining an uninvited guest in their hotel suite in Chicago. Finn Kelly had arrived early that morning with the news that he would be spending the day with them.

"Why? What's going on?" Michael Barlow asked.

Finn answered in his Irish accent. "Our mutual friend Tanner has reason to believe that Ordnance Inc. might choose this day to attack him. If that happens, you'll both be in a heap of trouble."

"You… you mean you'll kill us?" Kate asked.

Finn smiled at her. "If you weren't lying and there are no plans to attack, the three of us will spend a lovely day together." The smile left Finn's face. "If there is an attack planned and you know about it, speak up now."

"We don't know anything about an attack," Barlow said.

An expression of good humor returned to Finn's face. "Aye, that's what I wanted to hear. Now, let me see the room service menu; I'm hungry."

197

~

Not far from the Barlows' hotel, Trevor Healy entered Grayson Talbot's office and settled himself before the desk with a disgusted look on his face.

"Would you like to know what Tanner is doing today?"

"He's getting married at that ranch of his," Talbot said. "And don't look so shocked at my knowledge. Did you think I wouldn't keep track of the man's activities? Just because I'm biding my time in attacking him, it doesn't mean I've lost the desire for vengeance."

"I still don't see the need to wait, and to have attacked him on his wedding day would have been—"

"—utterly predictable." Talbot said. "Tanner is no fool and must have been expecting us to come at him, especially since you've placed the man on alert by using a surrogate against him."

"I've apologized for that, and the bastard paid me back for it. If I showed my face in New York City I'd likely be arrested for murder."

Talbot chuckled. "I have to give credit where credit is due, Tanner's handling of Blue Truth's investigation into him was masterful. The authorities are convinced that he's a fable. In the meantime, he's reclaimed his life and is building a future."

Healy jammed a finger against Talbot's desktop. "He shouldn't have a future, or a life, he should be crushed for what he did to our organization."

"Oh, he'll be crushed. When we do attack, we'll be an overwhelming force. It will make what happened to him as a boy pale in comparison. We'll annihilate him, Trevor, and we'll also strike when he's most vulnerable."

"How will we know when that moment arrives?"

Talbot's smile was icy. "We'll keep track of him, and, there's a spy in his camp."

"You've planted a spy?"

"It was only fair, since Tanner has inserted two in our ranks."

Healy rose from his seat. "Who are the traitors?"

"I'll explain, but first, I'll have our spy join us. It's time you two knew each other better."

Talbot sent a text on his phone, then he told Healy to mix drinks while they waited.

"What does our spy drink?"

"He'll settle for beer."

The intercom buzzed a moment after Healy returned to the desk, and Talbot told his assistant to, "Send him in."

When the door opened, Healy was looking at Billy Price.

"Price?"

Billy took a seat beside Trevor Healy and grabbed a bottle of beer.

"I see that Talbot has told you about me, Mr. Healy."

"You have a connection to Tanner?"

"Back when we were targeting him in Texas, he let me live if I killed a few people for him."

"What people?"

"It doesn't matter, Trevor," Talbot said. "What matters is that since that time, Tanner has been using Billy as a conduit into Ordnance Inc."

"And you've uncovered two other spies, Price?"

Billy nodded. "They must be spies, otherwise Tanner would have killed them long ago. I'm talking about the Barlows. I told Tanner that they were involved in digging up his family's graves, and he hasn't killed them. That tells me they're working for the man, just like he thinks I am."

Healy released a curse as his hands formed into fists.

"That's why they suddenly wanted to join us, and not stay independent. Michael and Kate are looking to find out when we plan to attack Tanner. Those sneaky... I'll have them tortured, then dumped into the lake like the garbage they are."

Talbot shook his head in an expression of disappointment. "Really? You want to kill the Barlows? Do you not see what an opportunity we have to send Tanner false information through them?"

Healy nodded, grudgingly. "Yes, you're right. It would be foolish to kill the Barlows before making use of them."

"And we will use them, by the time we attack Tanner, he'll think that we've decided to cut our losses where he's concerned. At the same time, we'll be coming at him when he's weakest."

Healy laughed. "I see why you can be so patient, Talbot; the more patient we are, the sweeter will be the victory."

"When we attack, nothing short of an army will stop us," Talbot said, and after speaking, he stood. "I've a flight to catch, but you two keep talking and make plans."

Healy told Price to follow him to his office, while Talbot grabbed his briefcase and headed out of the building.

GRAYSON TALBOT'S FLIGHT LANDED IN CALIFORNIA OVER five hours later. Thanks to the time difference he was able to make his dinner engagement with minutes to spare. Actually, he had arrived first, although a text informed him that his companion would be along at any moment.

When she appeared, The small blonde had the same effect on him that she always had, since the moment he'd first seen her. Talbot had fallen in love in an instant, and it had been a mutual experience.

Common sense told him he was courting disaster. He ignored any urge to stop seeing her, and in a short time, they had married.

After a passionate kiss of greeting, Talbot stared into his wife's eyes. "I've missed you, Amanda."

"I've missed you too, John," said FBI Agent Amanda Eriksen.

Eriksen had no idea who Grayson Talbot truly was, or what activities Solution Allies actually engaged in. She knew him by his real name and not the alias he used in his criminal activities. To Eriksen, Talbot was her cherished husband, a man who had saved her from a life of loneliness, where work was the only thing she'd lived for.

Grayson Talbot's real name was John Price. He was Billy Price's older brother.

EPILOGUE

A PRIVATE ISLAND IN FIJI

CODY AND SARA WERE HONEYMOONING IN PARADISE AND
had been at the exclusive resort for weeks. With only a few
days left before they were to head home to the ranch, they
had experienced almost everything the resort had to offer.
This included scuba diving, hiking, fishing, and a ride in a
personal submarine that could seat two. Above all else,
they had spent much of their time in bed together.

Sara had packed an item to take with her on the trip
that she had used moments earlier. She walked out of their
beachfront villa clad in a bikini and found Cody running
along the shoreline in a pair of red swim trunks. He was
brown from his time in the South Pacific sun, as was she.

When Cody spotted her, and viewed the expression on
her face, he halted his run, then turned toward her.

"Sara?"

She walked up to him with the item in her hand, then

held the plastic strip up for his inspection. When Cody realized what he was looking at, his grin was as wide as the sea.

"Really?"

Sara laughed with joy. "I'm pregnant."

TANNER RETURNS!

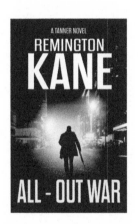

TANNER 25 - ALL-OUT WAR

AFTERWORD

Thank you,

REMINGTON KANE

JOIN MY INNER CIRCLE

You'll receive FREE books, such as,

SLAY BELLS – A TANNER NOVEL – BOOK 0

TAKEN! ALPHABET SERIES – 26 ORIGINAL TAKEN! TALES

BLUE STEELE - KARMA

Also – Exclusive short stories featuring TANNER, along with other books.

TO BECOME AN INNER CIRCLE MEMBER, GO TO:

http://remingtonkane.com/mailing-list/

ALSO BY REMINGTON KANE

The TANNER Series in order

The Young Guns Series in order

YOUNG GUNS

YOUNG GUNS 2 - SMOKE & MIRRORS

YOUNG GUNS 3 - BEYOND LIMITS

YOUNG GUNS 4 - RYKER'S RAIDERS

YOUNG GUNS 5 - ULTIMATE TRAINING

YOUNG GUNS 6 - CONTRACT TO KILL

YOUNG GUNS 7 - FIRST LOVE

YOUNG GUNS 8 - THE END OF THE BEGINNING

A Tanner Series in order

TANNER: YEAR ONE

TANNER: YEAR TWO

TANNER: YEAR THREE

TANNER: YEAR FOUR

TANNER: YEAR FIVE

The TAKEN! Series in order

TAKEN! - LOVE CONQUERS ALL - Book 1

TAKEN! - SECRETS & LIES - Book 2

TAKEN! - STALKER - Book 3

TAKEN! - BREAKOUT! - Book 4

TAKEN! - THE THIRTY-NINE - Book 5

TAKEN! - KIDNAPPING THE DEVIL - Book 6

TAKEN! - HIT SQUAD - Book 7

TAKEN! - MASQUERADE - Book 8

TAKEN! - SERIOUS BUSINESS - Book 9

TAKEN! - THE COUPLE THAT SLAYS TOGETHER - Book 10

TAKEN! - PUT ASUNDER - Book 11

TAKEN! - LIKE BOND, ONLY BETTER - Book 12

TAKEN! - MEDIEVAL - Book 13

TAKEN! - RISEN! - Book 14

TAKEN! - VACATION - Book 15

TAKEN! - MICHAEL - Book 16

TAKEN! - BEDEVILED - Book 17

TAKEN! - INTENTIONAL ACTS OF VIOLENCE - Book 18

TAKEN! - THE KING OF KILLERS – Book 19

TAKEN! - NO MORE MR. NICE GUY - Book 20 & the Series Finale

The MR. WHITE Series

PAST IMPERFECT - MR. WHITE - Book 1

HUNTED - MR. WHITE - Book 2

The BLUE STEELE Series in order

BLUE STEELE - BOUNTY HUNTER- Book 1

BLUE STEELE - BROKEN- Book 2

BLUE STEELE - VENGEANCE- Book 3

BLUE STEELE - THAT WHICH DOESN'T KILL ME- Book 4

BLUE STEELE - ON THE HUNT- Book 5

BLUE STEELE - PAST SINS - Book 6

BLUE STEELE - DADDY'S GIRL - Book 7 & the Series Finale

The CALIBER DETECTIVE AGENCY Series in order

CALIBER DETECTIVE AGENCY - GENERATIONS-
Book 1

CALIBER DETECTIVE AGENCY - TEMPTATION- Book 2

CALIBER DETECTIVE AGENCY - A RANSOM PAID IN
BLOOD- Book 3

CALIBER DETECTIVE AGENCY - MISSING- Book 4

CALIBER DETECTIVE AGENCY - DECEPTION- Book 5

CALIBER DETECTIVE AGENCY - CRUCIBLE- Book 6

CALIBER DETECTIVE AGENCY – LEGENDARY – Book 7

CALIBER DETECTIVE AGENCY – WE ARE GATHERED
HERE TODAY - Book 8

CALIBER DETECTIVE AGENCY - MEANS, MOTIVE, and
OPPORTUNITY - Book 9 & the Series Finale

THE TAKEN!/TANNER Series in order

THE CONTRACT: KILL JESSICA WHITE - Taken!/Tanner
- Book 1

UNFINISHED BUSINESS – Taken!/Tanner – Book 2

THE ABDUCTION OF THOMAS LAWSON -
Taken!/Tanner – Book 3

PREDATOR - Taken!/Tanner - Book 4

DETECTIVE PIERCE Series in order

MONSTERS - A Detective Pierce Novel - Book 1

DEMONS - A Detective Pierce Novel - Book 2

ANGELS - A Detective Pierce Novel - Book 3

THE OCEAN BEACH ISLAND Series in order

THE MANY AND THE ONE - Book 1

SINS & SECOND CHANES - Book 2

DRY ADULTERY, WET AMBITION -Book 3

OF TONGUE AND PEN - Book 4

ALL GOOD THINGS... - Book 5

LITTLE WHITE SINS - Book 6

THE LIGHT OF DARKNESS - Book 7

STERN ISLAND - Book 8 & the Series Finale

THE REVENGE Series in order

JOHNNY REVENGE - The Revenge Series - Book 1

THE APPOINTMENT KILLER - The Revenge Series - Book 2

AN I FOR AN I - The Revenge Series - Book 3

ALSO

THE EFFECT: Reality is changing!

THE FIX-IT MAN: A Tale of True Love and Revenge

DOUBLE OR NOTHING

PARKER & KNIGHT

REDEMPTION: Someone's taken her

DESOLATION LAKE

TIME TRAVEL TALES & OTHER SHORT STORIES

94315658R00132